MISSION TO THE UNKNOWN

Kana's attention was divided between the cliffs which walled in the stream bed and its flooring. Death might come suddenly from either direction. He was the one supposed to contact the opposition, but none of his training had prepared him for a situation such as this.

For Kana saw that before him were also bare mountains which showed no signs of life. You couldn't contact an enemy who wasn't there. But the Cos had devices which could kill at a distance. *And who could be sure that mountains showing no signs of life did not conceal the most powerful weapons of death?*

"Well-written, exciting . . . science-fiction fans and a good many other readers shouldn't miss!"

—*Boston Globe*

Fawcett Crest Books
by Andre Norton:

☐ THE JARGOON PARD   23615 $1.95

☐ JUDGMENT ON JANUS   24214 $1.95

☐ POSTMARKED THE STARS   24357 $2.25

☐ SHADOW HAWK   24186 $1.95

☐ SNOW SHADOW   23963 $1.95

☐ STAR RANGERS   24076 $1.95

☐ VELVET SHADOWS   23155 $1.95

☐ THE WHITE JADE FOX   24005 $1.95

☐ STAR MAN'S SON   23614 $1.95

Buy them at your local bookstore or use this handy coupon for ordering.

COLUMBIA BOOK SERVICE, CBS Publications
32275 Mally Road, P.O. Box FB, Madison Heights, MI 48071

Please send me the books I have checked above. Orders for less than 5 books must include 75¢ for the first book and 25¢ for each additional book to cover postage and handling. Orders for 5 books or more postage is FREE. Send check or money order only.

Cost $_____   Name _____

Sales tax*_____   Address _____

Postage_____   City _____

Total $_____   State _____ Zip _____

* *The government requires us to collect sales tax in all states except AK, DE. MT. NH and OR.*

This offer expires 1 April 82   8999

STAR GUARD

Andre Norton

FAWCETT CREST • NEW YORK

STAR GUARD

THIS BOOK CONTAINS THE COMPLETE TEXT OF
THE ORIGINAL HARDCOVER EDITION.

Published by Fawcett Crest Books, a unit of CBS Publications,
the Consumer Publishing Division of CBS Inc. by arrangement
with Harcourt Brace Jovanovich, Inc.

ISBN: 0-449-23646-3

Published in the United States of America

10 9 8 7 6 5 4 3

INTRODUCTION:
THE MERCENARIES

When the dominant species of a minor nine planet system revolving about a yellow sun known as "Sol"—situated close to the fringe of the Galaxy—gained knowledge of space flight and came out into our lanes of travel there arose a problem which Central Control had to solve, and speedily. These "men," as they called themselves, combined curiosity, daring, and technical skill with a basic will-to-compete against other races and species, an in-born thrust to conflict. Their answer to any problem was aggressive. Had this "will-to-battle" not been recognized at once for what it was and channeled into proper outlet, infinitesimal as their numbers were among us, we have been told that their influence might have torn asunder the peace of the stellar lanes and plunged whole sectors into war.

But the proper steps were taken at once and the Terrans were assigned a role which not only suited their nature but also provided a safety valve for all other belligerents among the systems which make up our great confederacy. Having been studied and carefully evaluated by Central Control psycho-techneers the Terrans were appointed to act as the mercenaries of the Galaxy—until such a time as these too independent and aggressive creatures would develop for themselves some less dangerous calling.

Thus there came into being the "Hordes" and "Legions" we find mentioned again and again in the various solar histories of the period. These organizations, manned by either "Archs" or "Mechs," carried on a formalized warfare for any planetary ruler who desired to enhance his prestige by employing them to fight his battles.

The Archs who comprised the Hordes were limited to service upon primitive worlds, being equipped with hand weapons and fighting in personal combat. The Mechs of the Legions followed technical warfare, indulging in it, however, more as a game in which it was necessary to make one's opponent concede victory, often without actual battle.

When still in the newly hatched stage "men" were selected to be either "Archs" or "Mechs" by rigid aptitude tests. After a period of intensive schooling in their trade they signed on for "enlistments" under field commanders. A portion of each payment made to the individual Horde or Legion commander by his employer was returned to their home world, Terra, as a tax. In other words, this system exported fighting men and the materials for war and became merchants of battle. Within a generation they accepted their role among us, apparently without question.

Three hundred years later (all students turn, please, to folio six, column two—the date of "3956 A.D." is a reckoning peculiar to Terra, we use it in your source material for this section because all reading will be based upon certain accounts written by the Terrans themselves) a minor Horde was employed by a rebellious native ruler on Fronn. While so engaged this organization uncovered a situation which changed history for their species, and perhaps for the Galaxy as well. Whether this change will operate for the general good for us all remains to be seen.

(*From a lecture in "Galactic History XX" delivered by Hist-Techneer Zorzi at the Galactic University of Zacan —Subject of the lecture: Minor Systems' Contribution to Historic Changes—presented first on Zol-Day, 4130 A.D. —Terran reckoning.*)

1

SWORDSMAN, THIRD CLASS

Because he had never been in Prime before Kana Karr, Arch Swordsman, Third Class, would have liked nothing better than to brace his lank length against the wall of the air port and stare up at those towers which fingered into the steely blue of the morning sky. But to do that was to betray himself as a greenie, so he had to be satisfied with ranking glances skyward to take in as much of the awesome sight as he could without becoming conspicuous. More than ever he was resentful of the fate which had delivered him at Combatant Headquarters a whole month later than his class of recruits, so that he would probably be the only newcomer among those waiting for assignment in the Hiring Hall.

Actually to be at Prime itself was exciting. This was the goal toward which ten years of intensive training had pointed him. He put down his war bag and rubbed his damp hands surreptitiously against the tight breeches which covered his thighs; though it was a crisp early spring day he was sweating. The stiff collar of his new green-gray tunic sawed at his throat and the cheek wings of his dress helmet chafed his jaws, while accouterments weighed more than they ever had before.

He was acutely conscious of the bare state of the belts crossing his shoulders, of the fact that his helmet was still crestless. The men who had shared the shuttle with him, those now in sight, scintillated with the gemmed loot of scores of successful missions, veterans every one of them.

Well—to achieve that status was only a matter of time, he repeated silently once more. Every one of these emblazoned figures now passing had stood there once, just as bare of insignia, probably just as uncertain inside as he now was—

Kana's attention was caught by another color, blazingly alive among the familiar waves of green-gray and silver. And his lips made a narrow line, his blue eyes, so startlingly vivid in his dark face, chilled.

A surface mobile had drawn up before the entrance of the very building to which he had been directed. And climbing out of it was a squat man swathed in a brilliant scarlet cloak, behind him two others in black and white. As if their arrival had been signaled, the Terran Combatants on the steps melted to right and left, making a wide path to the door.

But that was not in honor, Kana Karr reminded himself fiercely. Terrans on their home planet paid no deference to Galactic Agents, except in a style so exaggerated as to underline their dislike. There would surely come a time when—

His fists balled as he watched the red cloak and his guardian Galactic Patrolmen vanish inside the Hiring Hall. Kana had never had direct contact with an Agent. The X-Tees, the non-human Extra-Terrestrials, who had been his instructors after he had proved capable of absorbing X-Tee and Alien Liaison training, were a different class altogether. Perhaps because they were non-human he had never really ranked them among those rulers of Central Control who had generations earlier so blithely termed the inhabitants of Sol's system "barbarians," not eligible for Galactic citizenship except within the narrow limits they defined.

He was conscious that not all his fellows were as resentful of that as he was. Most of his classmates, for example, had been content enough to accept the future so arbitrarily decided for them. Outright rebellion meant the labor camps and no chance to ever go into space. Only a Combatant on military duty had the privilege of visiting the stars. And when Kana had learned that early in his career, he had set himself to acquire the shell of a model Arch, discovering in X-Tee training enough solace to aid his control of the seething hatred for the fact that he was not allowed to range the stars as he willed.

The sharp note of a military whistle proclaiming the hour brought him back to earth and the problem at hand. He shouldered his war bag and climbed the steps up which the Agent had gone a few moments before. He left his bag in the lockers by the door and took his place in the line of men winding into the inner hall.

The Mechs in their blue-gray coveralls and bubble helmets outnumbered the Archs in his particular section of that creeping line. And the few Archs near him were veterans. Consequently even when surrounded by his kind Kana felt as isolated here as he had in the street.

"They're trying to keep the lid on—but Falfa refused that assignment for his Legion." The Mech to his left, a man in his thirties with ten enlistment notches on his blade-of-honor, made no effort to keep his voice down.

"He'll get a board for refusing," returned his companion dubiously. "After all there's such a thing as a run of hard luck—"

"Hard luck? Two different Legions don't return from the same job and you talk about luck! I'd say that some investigating was called for. D'you know how many Legions have been written off the rolls in the past five years —twenty! Does that sound like bad luck?"

Kana almost echoed the other listener's gasp. Twenty Legions lost in battle over a period of five years—that *was* pushing the luck theory too far. If the modern, expertly armed Legions which operated only on civilized planets had been so decimated, what of the Hordes that served on barbarian worlds? Had their "luck" been equally bad? No wonder there had been a lot of undercover talk lately, comment that the price Central Control set on space—the price that Terra had paid for almost three hundred years —was too high.

The man before him moved suddenly and Kana hurried to close the gap between them. They were at the enlistment barrier. Kana pulled at the lock on his armlet to have it ready to hand to the Swordtan on duty there. That strip of flexible metal, fed into the record block, would automatically flash on the assignment rolls all the necessary information concerning one Kana Karr, Australian-Malay-Hawaiian, age eighteen and four months, training: basic with X-Tee specialization, previous service: none. And once that went into Hiring there was no turning back. The Swordtan took the band, allowed it to rest on the block for an instant, and handed it back with the lackluster boredom of one condemned to a routine job.

Within there were plenty of empty seats—Mechs to the lefts, Archs to the right. Kana slipped into the nearest seat and dared to stare about him. Facing the tiers of seats was the assignment board, already blinking orange signals and, although he knew his number could not possibly come up yet, he felt he must watch that steady stream of calls. Most seemed to be for the Mechs—sometimes four and five arose together and went through the door at the far end.

The Archs—Kana leaned forward in his seat to count the men on his side. At least twenty Swordsmen First Class, with even two Swordtans among them, were there. And fifty or more Second Class rankers. But—his eyes sought for other crestless helmets—he was the only Third Class man present. The recruits who had preceded him out of Training must have been hired before he came. Wait—red light—

Two S-2 men got up, settled their tunics with a twitch and adjusted their belts. But before they moved into the aisle there was an interruption. The board flashed white and then off entirely as a small party of men tramped down to ascend two steps to the announcement platform.

A Combatant, lacking the crossed shoulder belts of a field man, but with four stars shining on the breast of his tunic, stepped out to face the murmuring Swordsmen and Mechneers. He was flanked by the red-cloaked Galactic Agent and the latter's Patrolmen. Kana identified the three swiftly—humanoid. The Agent was a Vega Three native, the Patrolmen from Capella Two—the length of their slender legs unmistakable.

"Combatants!" the Terran officer's parade ground trained voice snapped out, to be followed by instant silence. "Certain recent events have made it necessary to make this announcement. We have made a full investigation—with the able assistance of Central Control facilities —into the trouble on Nevers. It is now certified that our defeat there was the result of local circumstances. The rumors concerning this episode are not to be repeated by any of the Corps—under the rule of loyalty—general code."

What in Terra! Kana's amazement might not be openly registered on the masklike face presented him by the blood of his Malay grandfather, but his mind raced. To make such a statement as that was simply asking for trouble—didn't the officer realize that? The Galactic Agent's frown proved that *he* wasn't pleased. Trouble on Nevers —this was the first he'd heard of it. But he'd wager half his first enlistment pay that within ten minutes every man in this hall would be trying to find out what were the rumors being so vigorously denied. It would spread like oil slick on a river.

The Agent stepped out, he appeared to be arguing with

the officer. But here he could only advise—he could not give direct orders. And it was too late to stop the damage now anyway. If he had made this move to allay fear, the Combatant officer had only given it fresh life.

With a decided shake of his head the officer started back down the aisle, the three others having, perforce, to follow him. Once more the lights flickered on the board. But the hum of talk rose to a gale of sound as soon as the door closed behind the quartette.

Kana's attention went back to the board just in time. Three more veterans had arisen on his own side of the hall, and, trailing their numbers, came the familiar combination he had answered to for the past ten years, almost more his name than the one his mixed island ancestry had given him.

Once through the other door he slackened pace, keeping modestly behind the rankers who had answered the same call. Third Class was Third Class and ranked nobody or nothing—except a cadet still in training. He was the lowest of the low and dared not presume to tread upon the heels of the man who had just stepped onto that lift.

The other was an Afric-Arab by his features—with maybe a dash of European blood bequeathed by one of the handful of refugees fleeing south during the atomic wars. He was very tall, and the beardless, dark skin of his face was seamed with an old scar. But the loot of many campaigns blazed from his helmet and belts and—Kana squinted against the light to be sure—there were at least half a dozen major notches on his rank sword, although he could not be very far into his thirties.

They lined up in an upper hallway, the Archs who had responded to that last call. And the veterans presented a brilliant array. Both Arch and Mech who served in the field off Terra were accustomed to carry their personal savings on their bodies. A successful mission meant another jewel added to the belt, or inset in the helmet. A lean season and that could be sold for credits to tide its owner over. It was a simple form of security which served on any planet in the Galaxy.

It was two minutes after twelve before Kana came inside the assignment officer's cubby. He was a badge Swordtan, with a plasta-flesh hand which explained his present inactive status. Kana snapped to attention.

"Kana Karr, Swordsman, Third Class, first enlistment, sir," he identified himself.

"No experience"—the plasta-flesh fingers beat an impatient tattoo on the desk top—"but you have X-Tee training. How far did you go?"

"Fourth level, Alien contact, sir." Kana was a fraction proud of that. He had been the only one in his training group to reach that level.

"Fourth level," the Swordtan repeated. From the tone he was not impressed at all. "Well, that's something. We're hiring for Yorke Horde. Police action on the planet Fronn. Usual rates. You en-ship for Secundus Base tonight, transship from there to Fronn. Voyage about a month. Term of enlistment—duration of action. You may refuse—this is a first choice." He repeated the last official formula with the weary voice of one who has said it many times before.

He was allowed two refusals, Kana knew, but to exercise that privilege without good reason gave one a black mark. And police action—while it covered a multitude of different forms of service—was usually an excellent way to get experience.

"I accept assignment, sir!" He pulled off his armlet for the second time and watched the Swordtan insert it in the block before him, pressing the keys which would enter on that band the terms of his first tour of duty. When he checked out at the end of the enlistment, a star would signify satisfactory service.

"Ship ups from Dock Five at seventeen hours. Dismissed!"

Kana saluted and left. He was hungry. The transients'

mess was open and being a combatant in service he was entitled to order more than just basic rations. But a dislike of spending pay he had not yet earned kept him to the plain fare he was allowed as long as he wore the Arch tunic. He lingered over the food, listening to the scraps of shop talk and rumor flying back and forth across the tables. As he had suspected the announcement made in the hiring hall had given birth to some pretty wild stories.

"Lost fifty legions in five years—" proclaimed one Mechtan. "They don't tell us the truth any more. I've heard that Longmead and Groth refused assignments—"

"The High Brass is getting rattled," commented a Swordtan. "Did you see old Poalkan giving us the fishy eye? He'd like to bring the Patrol in and mop up. Tell you what we ought to do—planet for some quiet in-fighting at a place I could name. That might help—"

There was a moment of silence. The speaker did not need to name his goal. All mankind's festering resentment against Central Control lay behind that outburst.

Kana could stall no longer. He left the hum of the mess hall. Yorke Horde was a small outfit. Fitch Yorke, its Blademaster, was young. He'd only had a command for about four years. But sometimes under young commanders you had better advancement. Fronn—that was a world unknown to Kana. But the answer to his ignorance was easy to find. He made his way through the corridors to a quiet room with a row of booths lining one wall. At the back of the chamber was a control board with banks of buttons. He pressed the proper combination of those and waited for the record-pak.

The roll of wire was a very thin one. Not much known of Fronn. He ducked into the nearest booth, inserted the wire in the machine there, and put aside his helmet to adjust the impression band on his temples. A second later he drifted off to sleep, the information in the pak being fed to his memory cells.

It was a quarter of an hour later when he roused. So

that was Fronn—not a particularly inviting world. And the pak had only sketched in meager details. But he now possessed all the knowledge the archives listed.

Kana sighed ruefully—that climate meant a tour in the pressure chamber during the voyage. The assignment officer had not mentioned that. Pressure chamber and water acclimate both. Serve him right for not asking more questions before he signed. He only hoped that he wasn't going to be sick for the whole trip.

When he went up to return the pak he met a Mechneer standing by the selector—an impatient Mech whistling tunelessly between his teeth, playing with the buckle of his blaster belt. He was only slightly older than Kana but he carried himself with the arrogant assurance of a man who had made at least two missions, an arrogance few real veterans displayed.

Kana glanced back at the booths. He had been the only occupant, so what was the Mech waiting there for? He dropped the pak on the return belt, but, as he reached the door, its polished surface reflected a strange sight. The Mech had scooped up the pak on Fronn before it vanished into the bin.

Fronn was a primitive world, a class five planet. Any Combatant force employed there must be, by Central Control regulations, an Arch Horde, trained and conditioned for so-called hand-to-hand fighting, their most modern weapon a stat-rifle. No mechanized unit would be sent to Fronn where their blasters, crawlers, spouters would be outlawed. So why should a Mech be interested in learning about that world?

Idle curiosity about planets on which one could not serve was not indulged among Combatants. It was about all one could do to absorb the information one could actually use.

Now Kana wished that he had had a closer look at the thin face which had been so shadowed by the bubble helmet. Puzzled and somewhat disturbed, he went on to the

commissary to lay in the personal supplies his new knowledge of Fronn suggested it wise to buy.

Wistfully he regarded and then refused a sleeping bag
of Ozakian spider silk lined with worstle temperature
moss. And the gauntlets of karab skin which the supply
corpsman tried to sell him were as quickly pushed aside.
Such luxuries were for the veteran with enough treasure
riding his belt to afford a buying spree. Kana must thriftily
settle for a second-hand Cambra bag—a short jacket of
Sasti hide, fur-lined and with a parka hood and gloves attached, and some odd medicament and toilet articles, in all
a very modest outfit which could easily be added to the
contents of his war bag. And when he settled the bill he
still had left four credits of his muster allowance.

The corpsman deftly rolled his purchases into a bundle.
"Looks like you're heading to some cold place, fella," he
commented.

"To Fronn."

The man grinned. "Never heard of the place. Back of
nowhere—sounds like to me. Look out they don't stick a
spear in you from behind some bush. Those nowhere guys
play rough. But then you guys do too, don't you?" He
stared knowingly at Kana's Arch uniform. "Yessir, kinda
rough, slugging it out the way you do. Me, I'd rather have
me a blaster and be a Mech—"

"Then you'd face another fighter with a blaster of his
own," Kana pointed out as he reached for the bundle.

"Have it your own way, fella." The corpsman lost interest as a be-jeweled veteran approached.

Kana recognized in the newcomer the man who had
preceded him to the assignment officer's cubby. Was he,
too, bound for Yorke Horde and Fronn? When the spider
silk sleeping bag was slapped down on the counter for his
inspection, and other supplies similar to Kana's modest selection piled on it, he was reasonably sure that guess was
correct.

At sixteen and a half hours the recruit stood beside his bag in the waiting section of Dock Five. So far he was alone save for the corpsmen who had business there and two spacer crewmen lounging at the far end. To have arrived so early was the badge of a greenie, but he was too excited under his impassive exterior to sit and wait elsewhere. It was twenty to seventeen before his future teammates began to straggle in. And ten minutes later they were swung up on the carry platform to the hatch of the troopship. Checking his armlet against the muster roll, the ship's officer waved Kana on. Within five minutes he entered a cabin for two, wondering which of the bunks was his to strap down on.

"Well"—a voice behind him exploded in a boom—"either get in or get out! This is no time to sleep on watch, recruit! Haven't you ever spaced before?"

Kana crowded back against the wall, snatching his bag away from the boots of the newcomer.

"Up there!" With an impatient snort his cabin mate pitched the younger man's bag up on the top bunk.

"Stow your gear in the compartment—there!" A brown thumb indicated the wall side of the bunk.

Kana swung up and investigated. Sure enough, a small knob twisted, and a section of the wall opened to display a recess which would accommodate his belongings. The rich note of a gong interrupted his exploration. At that signal the veteran loosened his belts and his helmet, putting them aside. And Kana hurriedly followed suit. One bong—first warning—

He stretched out on the bunk and fumbled for the straps which must be buckled. Under the weight of his body the foam pad spread a little. He knew that he could take acceleration—that was one of the first tests given a recruit in training. And he had been on field maneuvers on Mars and the Moon—but this was his first venture into deep space. Kana smoothed his tunic across his middle and waited for the third warning to announce the actual blastoff.

It had been a long time since Terrans had first reached toward other worlds. Three hundred years since the first recorded pioneer flight into the Galaxy. And even before that there were legends of other ships fleeing the atomic wars and the ages of political and social confusion which followed. They must have been either very desperate or very brave, those first explorers—sending their ships out into the unknown while they were wrapped in cold sleep with one chance in perhaps a thousand of waking as their craft approached another planet. With the use of Galactic overdrive such drastic chances were no longer necessary. But had his kind paid too high a price for their swifter passage from star to star?

Though a Combatant did not openly question the dictates of authority or the status quo, Kana knew that he was by no means alone in his discontent with Terra's role. What would have happened to his species if, when they had made that first historic flight, they had not met with the established, superior force of Central Control? According to their Galactic masters the potentials of the Terran mind, body and temperament fitted them for only one role in the careful pattern of space. Born with an innate will to struggle, they were ordered to supply mercenaries for the other planets. Because the C.C. psycho-techneers believed that they were best suited to combat, their planet and system had been arbitrarily geared to war. And Terrans accepted the situation because of a promise C.C. had made—a promise the fulfillment of which seemed farther in the future every year—that when they were ready for a more equal citizenship it would be granted them.

But what if Central Control had not existed? Would the Agents' repeated argument have proved true? Would the Terrans, unchecked, have pulled planet after planet into a ruthless struggle for power? Kana was sure that was a lie. But now, if a Terran wanted the stars, if the desire for new and strange knowledge burned in him—he could buy it only by putting on the Combatant's sword.

A giant hand squeezed Kana's rib case against laboring lungs. He forgot everything in a fight for breath. They had blasted off.

2

FIRST TESTING

Kana must have blacked out, for when he was again aware of his surroundings he saw that his cabin mate was maneuvering across their quarters, getting his "space legs" in the weak gravity maintained in the living sections of the ship. Lacking his helmet, his tunic open halfway down his broad chest, the veteran had lost some of his awe-inspiring aura. He might now be one of the hard-visaged instructors Kana had known for more than half his short life.

Space tan on a naturally dark skin made him almost black. His coarse hair had been shaved and trimmed into the ridge scalp lock favored by most Terrans. He moved with a tell-tale feline litheness and Kana decided that he would not care to match swords with him in any point-free contest. Now he turned suddenly as if sensing Kana's appraising stare.

"Your first enlistment?" he snapped.

Kana wormed free of the straps which imprisoned him and dangled his feet over the edge of the bunk before he replied.

"Yes, sir. I'm just up from Training—"

"Lord, they send 'em out young these days," commented the other. "Name and rank—"

"Kana Karr, sir, Swordsman, Third Class."

"I'm Trig Hansu." There was no reason for him to proclaim his rank, the double star of a Swordtan was plain on his tunic. "You signed for Yorke?"

"Yes, sir."

"Believe in beginning the hard way, eh?" Hansu jerked a jump seat from its wall hollow and sat down. "Fronn's no garden spot."

"It's a start, sir," Kana returned a bit stiffly and slipped down to the deck without losing a one-hand hold on the bunk.

Hansu grinned sardonically. "Well, we're all heroes when we're first out of Training. Yorke's a trail hitter and a jumper. You have to be con to keep up in one of his teams."

Kana had a defense ready for that. "The assignment officer asked for a recruit, sir."

"Which can mean several things, youngster, none of them complimentary. S-Threes come cheaper on the payroll than Ones or Twos—for example. Far be it from me to disillusion the young. There's mess call. Coming?"

Kana was glad that the veteran had given him that invitation, for the small mess hall was crowded with what seemed to his bedazzled eyes nothing but high ranks. There was gravity enough so that one could sit in a civilized fashion and eat—but Kana's stomach did not enjoy the process any. And soon such sensations would be worse, he thought grimly, when he had to go through pressure conditioning before landing on Fronn. He regarded the noisy crowd about him with a growing depression.

A Horde was divided into teams and teams into doubles. If a man didn't find a double on his own but was arbitrarily paired by his commander with a stranger, some of the few pleasures and comforts of Combat field service were automatically endangered. Your double fought, played, and lived by your side. Often your life depended upon his skill and courage—just as his might upon yours.

Doubles served years of enlistments together, moving in a firmly cemented partnership from one Horde or Legion to another.

And who in this glittering gang would choose to double with a greenie? The situation would probably end by his being assigned to a veteran who would resent his inexperience and provide him with the makings of a tough jump right from the start. Waugh—he *was* getting space blues tonight! Time to change think-tracks for sure.

But that subtle unease which haunted him all that long and eventful day lingered, coming to a head in a strange and horrifying dream in which he ran breathlessly across a shadow landscape trying to avoid the red ray of a Mech blaster. He awoke with a choked gasp and lay sweating in the darkened cabin. Hunted by a Mech—but Mechs did not fight against Archs. Only—it was some time before he was able to sleep again.

The beams of the ship's artificial day brought him to life much later. Hansu was gone, the contents of his war bag spilled out on his empty bunk. A wicked needle knife, its sheath polished smooth by long wear against the bare skin of its owner's inner arm, caught Kana's eye. Its unadorned hilt was designed for service. And its presence among the gear meant that Kana was now sharing the quarters of a man practiced in the deadliest form of Combatant in-fighting. The recruit longed to pick it up, test its perfect balance and spring for himself. But he knew better than to touch another's personal weapons without the express permission of the owner. That act to his fellows was a direct insult which could lead only to a "meeting" from which one of them might never return. Kana had heard enough tall tales from the instructors at Training to make him familiar with the barracks code.

He was a late arrival at mess and ate with apologetic speed under the impatient eye of the stewards. Afterwards he went on to the small lounge deck where the Combatants sprawled at leisure. There was a card game in progress, and the usual circle of intent players about a Yano board. But Trig Hansu was a member of neither group. Instead he sat cross-legged on a mat pad, a portable reader before him, watching the projection of a pak.

Curious, Kana edged between the gamesters to see the tiny screen. He caught sight of a fraction of landscape, dark, gloomy, across which burden-bearing creatures moved from left to right. Hansu spoke without turning his head.

"If you're so curious, greenie, squat."

Feeling as hot as a rocket's tail Kana would have melted away but Hansu pushed the machine to the right in real invitation.

"Our future." He jerked a thumb at the unwinding scene as the recruit dropped to his knees to watch. "That's a pak view of Fronn."

The marchers on the Fronnian plain were quadrupeds, their stilt legs seemingly only skin drawn tightly over bone. Packs rested on either side of their ridged spines and knobby growths fringed their ungainly necks and made horn excrescences on their skulls.

"Caravan of guen," Kana identified. "That must be the west coastal plains."

Hansu pressed a stud on the base of the reader and the screen blanked out. "You asked for indoctrination on Fronn?"

"From the archives, sir."

"The enthusiasms of the young have their points. And you're just out of Training. Specialization—knife— rifle—?"

"Basic in everything, sir. But specialization in X-Tee— Alien Liaison mostly—"

"Hmm. That would explain your being here." Hansu's comment seemed obscure. "X-Tee— I wonder what they spring on you in that nowadays. What about—" He swung sharply into a series of questions, delivered rapid fire, which were certainly very close in their searching value to what Kana had faced back in Training before he had been granted his mark of proficiency. When he had answered them to the best of his ability—having to say frankly, far too many times, "I don't know"—he saw Hansu nod.

"You'll do. Once you get a lot of that theory knocked out of your head, and let experience teach you what you should really know about this game, you'll be worth at least half your pay to a Blademaster."

"You said that X-Tee specialization explained my assignment, sir—?"

But the veteran appeared to have lost interest in the conversation. The Yano game broke up in a noisy if good-natured argument, and Hansu was tapped on the shoulder by one of his own rank and urged into the group reforming for a second round.

And because he had not answered that question Kana began to note more carefully the caliber of the men about him. These were not only veterans, but long-service men with a high percentage of stars. The scraps of conversation he overheard mentioned famed commanders, Hordes with long lists of successful engagements. Yet Fitch Yorke was a comparative newcomer, with no fame to pull in such men. Wouldn't it have been more normal for them to refuse enlistment under him? Why the concentration of experience and skill in an obscure Horde on an unknown planet? Kana was certain that Hansu, for one, was an outstanding X-Tee expert—

But during the next few days he saw little of the veteran, and the landing on Secundus after the boredom of the trip could not come soon enough.

The temporary quarters assigned to Yorke's men was a long hall, one end of which was a mess station while the other was tiered with bunks. With a hundred men dragging in supplies and personal equipment, greeting old comrades, sharing Horde rumor and Combat news, the room was a hurricane of noise and confusion. Kana, not knowing just where to go, followed Hansu down the length of the room. But when the Swordtan turned to join a glittering circle of his peers, the recruit was left to hunt a dim corner suitable to his inexperience and general greenness.

There was not much choice. The S-Threes congregated in the least desirable section by the door. And with a sense of relief Kana noted several whose uniforms were as bare of ornament as was his own. He tramped over and claimed a top bunk by tossing his war bag up on its pad.

"D'you see who just mustered in?" one of his neighbors demanded of the young man beside him. "Trig Hansu—!"

A low whistle of astonishment became words. "But he's top brass! What's he doing in this outfit? He could claim shares with Zagren Osmin or Franlan. Yorke should be flattered to get the time of day from him."

"Yeah? Well, I've heard he's queer in some ways. He'll cut a top outfit any time to get off the regular travel lanes and visit a new world. He's space whirly over exploring. Could have had a Horde of his own long ago if he hadn't always been jumping off into the black. And, besides, brother, haven't noticed something else about this particular crowd? Yorke's snaffled himself more than one big name in this pull-out. Hello—" He noticed Kana's bag and now he turned smartly to survey its owner.

"So—something new on the rocket's tail. A nice greenie out to make his fortune or die on the field of glory. What's your name and condition, greenie?"

There was no bite of sarcasm in that demand and the speaker did not outrank Kana very far in either years or service.

"Kana Karr, S-Three—"

"Mic Hamet, S-Three—that clay-clawer resting his sore feet over there is Rey Nalassie, also of our lowly rank. First assignment?"

Kana nodded. Mic Hamet's dark red hair was roached in the scalp ridge, but his unusually fair skin was reddened rather than tanned by exposure and there was a spattering of freckles across his somewhat flat nose. His friend un-

coiled long legs and rose to a gangling six-foot-two, his
lantern-jawed face solemn, though his sleepy gray eyes
displayed humor and interest.

"They scraped us out of a rotation depot. We had bad
luck a while back. Rey got bit by a bug during our last
stretch and we had to default out of Oosterbeg's Horde
four months short. So we were flat enough in the purse to
sign on here when the assign officer looked at us as if we
were slightly better than muck worms."

"You doubled yet, Karr?" asked Nalassie in a husky
voice.

"No, I was delayed in leaving Training. And all the fellows who shipped out of Prime with me were vets—"

Mic lost his half grin. "That's tough luck. Most of us
Threes are paired already and you wouldn't want to double with either Krosof or the rest—"

"Heard tell that if you come in solo, Yorke puts you
with a vet," Rey volunteered. "Got a theory youth should
be tamed by age—or something of the sort."

"And that's worse than tough," broke in his partner.
"You shouldn't team up with anyone until you know him.
I'd play it single as long as I could, if I were you, Karr.
You might be lucky enough to find some good fella who's
lost his partner. Stick with us until you do double if you
want to—"

"And a very good way to stay out of trouble with the
jeweled ones"—Rey nodded toward the rankers' side of
the hall—"is to get out of here." He put on his helmet and
buckled the chin strap. "They aren't going to muster until
morning, we can still have a night on the town. And, fella,
you haven't seen excitement until you've seen the leave
section of Secundus."

Kana was enthusiastic until he thought of the leanness
of his purse. Four credits wouldn't even pay for a meal in
a base town—he was sure of that. But, as he shook his
head, Mic's fingers closed on his arm.

"No quibbling, fella. We'll be a long time in the back

country and we aren't comfortable, shipping out with credits sticking to our fingers. We'll stand you—then when you get your first star, you can repay in kind—that's fair enough. Now, quick about it, before someone gets the idea of putting the younger generation to labor for the good of their souls!"

Beyond the walls of the Combat area a typical leave town had grown up. Taverns, cafes, gambling establishments catered for all ranks and purses, from Blademasters and Mecmasters to recruits. It was certainly no place to visit with only four credits, Kana thought again as he blinked at the light of the gaudy signs lining the street before them.

And, to his discomfort, the ideas of his guides were not modest. They steered him by the cafes he would have chosen and dragged him through a wide door where Terran gold-leaf was overlaid with the sea-green shimmer of Trafian scale lac. Their boots pressed flat the four-inch pile of carpets which could only have been woven on Caq, and the walls were cloaked with the tapestries of Sansifar. Kana balked.

"This is strictly a glitter boy's shop," he protested. But Mic's hold on him did not relax and Rey chuckled.

"No rank off field," Mic reminded him sardonically. "S-Threes and Blademasters—we're all the same in our skins. Only civilians worry about artificial distinctions—"

"Sure. In Combat you go where you please. And we please to come here." Rey sniffed the scented air which stirred the shining arras, shaking the figures on them to quivering life. "By the Forked Tail of Blamand, what I wouldn't give to be in on the sacking of this! And here comes mine host's assistant."

The figure loping toward them was one of the skeleton-lean, big-headed natives of Wolf II. He greeted them with a professional smile, disclosing the double row of fangs which tended to make Terrans slightly nervous, and inquired their pleasure in a series of ear-taxing growls.

"Nothing big," Mic returned. "We have muster tomorrow. Suppose you let us trot around by ourselves, Feenhalt. We won't get into trouble—"

The Lupian's pointed grin widened as he waved them on. When they passed through a slit in the curtain to the next room Kana commented:

"I take it you're known here?"

"Yes. We got Feenhalt out of a hole once. He isn't a bad old Wolf. Now—let's mess."

They escorted Kana through a series of rooms, each exotic in its furnishings, each bizarrely different, until they came to a chamber which brought a surprised exclamation out of him. For they might have stepped into a section of jungle. Gigantic fern-trees forested the walls and looped long fronds over their heads, but did not exclude a golden light which revealed cushioned benches and curving tables. Among the greenery swooped and fluttered streaks of flaming color which could only be the legendary Krotands of Cephas' inner sea islands. Kana, meeting such travelers' tales in truth, bemusedly allowed his companions to push him down on a bench.

"Krotands? But how—?"

Mic's knuckles rapped and drew a metallic answer from the bole of the fern tree immediately behind them. Kana reached out to find that his fingers slid over a solid surface instead of rough bark. They were in a clever illusion.

"All done with mirrors," Mic assured him solemnly. "Not that it isn't one of the best bits of projecting Slanal ever designed. Feenhalt's got the business head—but it's his boss who thought up this sort of thing. Ha—food."

Plates arose out of the table top. Warily Kana tasted and then settled down to hearty stoking.

"It'll be a long time before we get another feed like this," Rey observed. "I heard Fronn's no pleasure planet."

"Cold to our notion—and the native culture is feudal," Kana supplied.

" 'Police action,' " mused Mic. "Police action doesn't

match a feudal government. What is the set-up—kings? Emperors?"

"Kings—they call them 'Gatanus'—ruling small nations. But their heirship is reckoned through the female line. A Gatanu is succeeded by his eldest sister's son, not his own. He is considered closer kin to his mother and sisters than to his father or brothers."

"You must have studied up on this—"

"I used a record pak at Prime."

Rey looked pleased. "You're going to be an asset. Mic, we've got to keep our paws on this one."

Mic swallowed a heroic bite. "We sure have. Somehow I am visited by a feeling that this jump is not going to be foam-pad riding, and the more we know, the better for us."

Kana glanced from one to the other, catching the shadow glimpse of trouble. "What's up?"

Mic shook his head and Rey shrugged. "Blasted if we know. But—well, when you've trotted around the back of beyond and poked into places where a 'man' is a mighty queer animal, you get a feeling about things. And we have a feeling about this—"

"Yorke?"

The morale of any Horde depended upon the character of its Blademaster. If Yorke could not inspire confidence in those who followed him—

Mic frowned. "No, it's not Fitch Yorke. By all accounts he's a master to latch to. There have been a lot of the glitter boys beside Hansu sign up for this jump—you can always tell by that how a Blademaster stacks. It's a feeling —you get it sometimes—a sort of crawling—inside you—"

"Somebody kicking at your grave mark," Rey contributed.

Mic's big mouth twisted in a grin aimed at himself. "Regular mist wizards, aren't we? Step right up—read your future for a credit! Fronn isn't going to be any worse than a lot of other places I know. Through? Then let's show our greenie Feenhalt's private rake-off. Only time the old Wolf showed any imagination—And, Space Bats, does it ever pay off!"

Feenhalt's flight of imagination turned out to be a gambling device which enthralled a large selection of Combatants. A pool sunk in the floor of a room was partitioned into sections around a central arena. In each of the small water-filled pens sported a fish about five inches long, two-thirds of that length mouth lined with needle teeth. Each fish bore a small colored tag imbedded in its tail fin and swam about its prison in ferocious fury. The players gathered about the pool studying the captives. When two or more had chosen their champions, credit chips were inserted in the slots on the rim and the pen doors opened, freeing the fish to move into the arena. What followed was a wild orgy of battle until only one warrior remained alive. Whereupon the bettor who had selected that fish collected from those who had sponsored the dead.

No more attractive game could have been devised to snare credits from Combatants. Kana measured the twisting finny fighters carefully, at last choosing a duelist with an excellent jaw spread and a green tail disc. He bought a credit chip from the house banker and knelt to insert the releasing coin in the lock of the pen.

A meaty, hair-matted hand splayed against his shoulder and Kana only caught himself from landing in the pool with a back-wrenching twist.

"Outta th' way, little boy. This here's for men—"

"Just what—!" Kana's words ended in a cough as Mic's fist landed between his shoulders and someone else jerked him away from the man who had taken his place and his fish. The fellow grinned up at him maliciously. Then, as if he expected no more trouble, he turned back to encourage the fighter released by the recruit's chip.

All the good humor was gone from Mic's face and even

Rey's dancing eyes were sober as they moved Kana away, holding him motionless between them in an "unarmed infighting" grip against which he knew better than to struggle.

"We blast—now—" Mic informed him.

"Just what"—he began again—"do you think—"

"Fella, you might have dug your own grave there. That was Bogate—Zapan Bogate. He has twenty duel notches on his sword—eats greenies for breakfast when he can get them." Mic's words were light but his voice deadly serious.

"Do you think I'm afraid—" Kana smarted.

"Listen, fella, there's a big difference between being prudent and alive, and kicking a Martian sand mouse in the teeth. You don't last long after the latter heroic deed. You can't be given a yellow stripe for ducking a run-in with Bogate—you're just intelligent. Someday one of the big boys—Hansu or Deke Mills or somebody like that—is going to get annoyed with Bogate. Then—man, oh, man —you'll be able to sell standing room at the fracas to half the forces and be a billion-credit man! Bogate is sudden and painful death on two crooked feet."

"Besides being about the best scout who ever sniffed a trail," cut in Rey. "Bogate at play and Bogate in the field are two different characters. The Blademasters tolerate the one on account of the other."

Kana recognized truth when he heard it. To return and tackle Bogate was stupid. But he still protested until they were interrupted by Hansu. The veteran, followed by two base policemen, bore down upon them.

"Yorke men?" he asked.

"Yes, sir."

"Report to Barracks—on the quick. Blast-off has been moved up—" He was already past them to round up more of the Horde.

The three started back to the Combat area at a trot.

"Now what?" Rey wanted to know. "Last I heard we upped ship at noon tomorrow. Why all the hurry? We haven't even had muster line yet."

"I told you," grunted Mic, "that there was a smell about this—not perfume either. Octopods! That dinner we downed—and pressure chamber conditioning coming up! We're going to be mighty sorry we ate, mighty sorry."

With this dire prophecy still ringing in his ears Kana collected his war bag from the bunk he had not had a chance to occupy and took his place with Mic and Rey on the hoist platform to be slung on board the transport. Counted off by fours Kana found himself sharing a pressure chamber with his two new acquaintances and a supply man—the latter obviously bored by his juvenile company. They stripped to their shorts, submitted to shots from the medico. And then there was nothing left to do but strap down on the bunks and endure the ensuing discomfort.

The next few days were anything but pleasant. Slowly their bodies were forced to adapt to Fronn, since the planet was *not* going to adapt to them. It was a painful process. But when they landed on that chill world they were ready for action.

Kana still lacked a double. He clung to Mic and Rey as they had advised, but he knew that sooner or later that threesome must be broken and he would be assigned a partner. He was shy of the veterans, and the three or four other S-Threes who were not yet paired for muster-line were not the type he desired to know better. Most of them were older men with experience who were incorrigible enough to remain permanently in the lowest ranks. Good in the field, they were troublemakers in barracks and had shifted from one Horde to another at the end of each enlistment with the relieved sighs of those who had just served wafting them on their separate ways. Kana continued to hope that he would not draw one of them as a double.

The Terrans' first sight of Fronn was disappointing. They planeted at dusk, and, since Fronn was moonless, marched through darkness to the squat, rough-hewn stone building which was to serve them as temporary barracks. There were no fittings at all in the long room and the three sat on their war bags, wondering whether to unroll sleeping bags or wait for further instructions.

Rey's long nose wrinkled in disgust as he moved his boots from a suspicious stain on the dirty floor. "I'd say we got this place second hand—"

"Second hand?" Mic asked. "Closer fifth. And most of the others before us were animals. This is a Fronnian cow barn if my nose doesn't deceive me."

The call Kana had been dreading came at last, doubles were to register at the table a Swordtan had set up at the far end of the room. Rey and Mic, after a word of encouragement, got in line.

Kana hesitated, not knowing just what to do, when the harsh rasp of a new voice startled him. Zapan Bogate and another of the same type had fallen into line near him. A third of their pattern stood beside Bogate grinning.

"Jus' a greenie—don't know what to do next. Pore little lost greenie. You, Sim, go and take him by the hand. He needs his nurse—"

Kana tensed. With Bogate's encouragement Sim shuffled forward, his brutal face twisted in a wry grimace he might have intended as a smile.

"Pore little greenie," Bogate repeated, his voice rising so that half the line were turning to see the sport. "Sim's gonna look after him, ain't you, Sim?"

"Sure am, Zap. Come along, greenie—" His hairy paw caught Kana's sleeve.

What followed was mostly sheer reflex action on the recruit's part. The disgust which that touch aroused in him triggered his move. His hand chopped down across the other's wrist, striking the hand from its hold. As Sim gog-

gled, Bogate stepped out of line, his small eyes gleaming
with sadistic joy.

"Seems like the greenie don't favor you, Sim. Whatta
we do to greenies who don't know what's good for them?"

Kana thought he was alert but Sim surprised him. He
had not expected the hulking bully to follow code custom.
Sim's slap across his face had power enough to swing him
half around, blinking back tears of pain. As he regained
his balance Kana's mind was working feverishly. Barracks
duel—just the sort of encounter these bullies wanted—le-
gal enough so no watching Combatant would dare to inter-
fere.

He had a single advantage. They would expect him to
choose the usual weapons—swords with shielded points.
Thanks to his study of the record-pak on Terra he had an
answer which would give him a chance to escape a nasty
mauling.

He and Sim were now surrounded by a circle of expec-
tant spectators. Kana tasted the sweet flatness of blood
from the lip the other's slap had scraped against his teeth.

"Meet?" Automatically he asked the proper question.

"Meet."

"Give me your sword, Sim. I'll cap it for you," Bogate
ordered genially.

"Not so fast." Kana was glad that his voice sounded so
even and unhurried. "I didn't say swords—"

Bogate's grin faded, his eyes narrowed. "Yeah? Guns is
out—not on active service, greenie."

"I choose bat sticks," returned Kana.

A moment of utter and uncomprehending silence was
his first answer.

3

FORWARD MARCH

Those Archs who had been longer on Fronn began to understand, though Sim apparently did not. As he glanced to Bogate asking for direction, Hansu elbowed his way into the center of the circle. Behind him was another man, much younger, but bearing himself with the same unselfconscious authority.

"You heard him," Hansu said to Sim. "He's chosen bat sticks. And you'll meet here and now. We want this over before we march out."

Sim was still bemused and, seeing that, Kana began to hope. Blunted swords were one thing—a man could be maimed or even killed when he faced an expert in such warfare. But armed with one of those wands made of a highly poisonous wood which left seared welts on human skin—the whips used by Fronnian caravan men to subdue the recalcitrant guen—he had a chance, and maybe more than just an even one.

Kana unbuckled his helmet strap and found Mic's hand ready to receive the headgear as he discarded it. Rey edged up to help him unfasten his cross belts.

"Know what you're doing, fella?" he asked in a half whisper as Kana shed his tunic.

"Better than Sim does, I think," Kana returned, peeling off his shirt.

His first little spark of hope was growing into steady confidence. Sim was still confused and Bogate's grin had been wiped from his ugly face. The young man who had followed Hansu disappeared. But before Kana had time to shiver in the chill of the unheated building he was back, carrying in gloved hands two of the bright crimson bat sticks. Seeing what he held, those who knew Fronn gave him quick room.

Kana drew on a gauntlet and gripped the nearest stick. They were of equal weight and reach. And, as the circle of spectators moved out to give them room, the recruit believed that Sim's battered face now registered a certain uneasiness.

They came on guard at command, using the canes as they would the heavier and more familiar steel. But where a duelist must fear only the blunted point of the sword, here the slightest touch would bring pain. Their boots made faint whispering sounds as they circled, the sticks meeting with a thud as they thrust and parried.

Kana, after the third pass, knew that he was facing a master swordsman, but he also guessed that the relative lightness of this strange weapon was bothering Sim and that his opponent was not quite sure of himself or aware of the potentialities of the cane he wielded.

There was a single stroke which would put an end to the duel. Kana wondered if Sim realized that. A raking sweep across arm muscles—the resulting pain would make that limb useless for minutes. He concentrated on achieving that, his world narrowed to the cane he was using and the swaying, dodging body before him. Sim had abandoned the more obvious attacks and was settling down to a semi-defensive action, apparently content to leave experimentation to Kana, thereby displaying more shrewdness than Kana had credited to him.

With none of his confidence shaken, but more warily,

Kana circled—using the traditional thrusts and parries which were a beginner's. Sim must be drawn into the open in the belief that he faced a novice.

Something struck him in the short ribs and glanced along his flesh. It brought with it a blaze of agony almost as bad as a blaster burn. Kana set his teeth as, encouraged by that scoring, Sim's defense changed to an attack the recruit found hard to meet. He was forced back, giving ground willingly enough with a single aim in mind—to reach that point on the muscled arm before him.

· Sim's cane got home again, up the angle of Kana's jaw. The younger man shook his head dazedly, but a leap back bought him a moment in which to pull himself together. That sharp retreat must have given Sim the idea that his opponent's nerve was breaking, for now he bored in with a wild whirlwind of blows. There came the moment Kana had waited for, his cane drew a torturing line across Sim's sword arm just below the shoulder. And, more unprepared than Kana had been, the older man cried out, clawing at the red welt, his cane rolling across the floor to strike against Kana's boot. The recruit brought his stick up in formal salute.

"Satisfied?" He asked the traditional question.

Sim was speechless with pain as he nodded, though the hatred in his small eyes fought with the agony of his hurt. Since he could no longer hold his weapon he must concede, but he was far from satisfied.

. Kana became aware of the buzz of talk about them. Snatches of conversation informed him that these connoisseurs were discussing his exploit from every possible angle. He dropped his cane to the floor and raised his hand to the burn on his jaw.

"Don't touch that, you young fool!" snapped the voice of authority. The young man who had provided the canes pushed Kana's hand away and began dabbing delicately at the welt with a yellow grease. As it spread across the reddened skin Kana felt a coolness draw out the fire. He stood patiently while they doctored the slash on his side and then shrugged into the shirt Mic brought him.

"All right, all right!" Hansu's deep growl cut through and across the din. "The show's over—"

But as the others shuffled back into line the Swordtan stood between Kana and Sim, eyeing them both with a steel-based coldness. "For brawling in barracks," he announced, "three days' field pay fine! And if either of you have any clever ideas about trying it again—you'll deal with me!"

Kana, unable to don his helmet because of his jaw, gave ready agreement to keep the peace, and Sim's mumble was also accepted.

"You—Lozt, go in with Daw." Hansu jerked a thumb to the end of the line. And Sim, nursing his limp arm, obediently passed Bogate to take the indicated place beside a dark, wiry veteran. Kana remained where he was.

"I'll answer for this one," the younger veteran spoke up and Kana sensed that this had been decided between his two superiors. Still uninformed as to who his partner was, he followed along.

"Mills and Karr," Hansu set them down together on the muster roll as members of the team he himself commanded.

"Mills"—there was something familiar in that name. Kana went back to claim his bag trying to recall where he had heard it before and ran into a highly excited Mic and an equally amazed Rey.

"Let me touch you," Mic greeted him. "Maybe some of that luck will rub off. I can sure use it!"

"You must have been born with a sword in your hand and a star in your mouth!" contributed Rey. "How do you rate Deke Mills for a double, greenie?"

Deke Mills! Again that name almost rang a gong, but still he couldn't remember.

"Great Blades!" Mic's eyes and mouth were circles of astonishment. "I don't believe he knows what has hap-

pened to him! Somebody ought to teach greenies the facts
of life before they ship them out into the cruel, cold world.
Deke Mills, fella, is a star-double-star. He's nudging people like Hansu for top honors. Space, he could have his
pick of doubles out of the whole Horde! He might have
partnered Hansu if Yorke hadn't insisted that Trig command a team."

Kana swallowed. "But why——" His mouth was suddenly
dry.

"Not for your pretty blue eyes anyway," Mic told him.
"He was unattached and so were you. Yorke's rule is a vet
with a greenie where there's last minute choosing to be
done. You're lucky in that you were at the right place at
the right time. Lucky, you're dripping with the stuff!"

"I'd rather stay with you two." Kana spoke the truth.
To double with a notable such as Deke Mills was the last
thing he wished. He would do everything wrong, and all
his mistakes would be magnified in such exalted company.
At that moment he would almost rather have walked beside Sim.

"Cheer up." Mic grinned. "We're in the same team.
And Mills is acting as one of Hansu's aides—you may not
see too much of him after all."

"Better cut along," warned Rey. "There's Mills by the
door. Don't keep him waiting."

Kana scooped up his bag, wincing as he moved his
head. Yes, the young veteran stood by the door talking to
a handful of rankers. Kana hurried, beginning to wish that
he had used his privilege and refused this assignment.

It was close to midnight, ship time, when he joined
Mills. Outside there were rays of a dull bluish light, weak
and dim to Terran eyes. Kana gathered that instead of remaining in the odorous barn for the night the Combatants
were moving out of the Fronnian town to the camp site the
first comers had established.

The street was roughly paved and drawn up there was a
line of light, two-wheeled carts. Each was pulled by a gu

—most of which were bubbling ill temperedly—granted plenty of room by the alien soldiers. As Kana followed Mills' example and tossed his bag into the leading cart he passed close to the first Fronnian he had seen in the flesh.

This was a Llor, one of the dominant race on the continental land masses. Humanoid in general appearance the native stood a good seven feet. In a climate where the Terrans were glad to wear double-lined winter clothing, the Llor was bare to the waist. But nature had provided him with a coat of thick curly hair, close in texture to the wool of a sheep, from which came a pungent, oily odor only apparent to those from off world. This hairy covering was thinner on the face—an odd face to non-Llor eyes for the nose was bridgeless and represented by a single nostril slit, while the eyes bulged from their round sockets in a singularly disconcerting stare. The mouth was small and round, and if the Llor possessed any teeth they were not visible. His only garment, save for a harness which supported a sword and a hand gun, was a short kilt made of strips of tanned hide, each hardly wider than a thread of fringe. Boots with pointed toes, the tips of which were capped with wicked metal spikes, were laced to his knees.

As the Combatants loaded their baggage aboard the cart the Llor lounged at ease, chewing on a section of purple-blue cane and spitting noisily at intervals. When the bags of six men had been piled on the vehicle he tended, he straightened, prodded the snarling gu with a bat stick and the cart creaked on, the Terrans falling in behind.

Blue lamps fastened to the blank, windowless walls of the structures they passed afforded enough light to march along the street, but the footing was rough.

"This is Tharc, capital city of Skura's province." Mills' voice rose over the clatter made by the metal wheels of the cart. "Skura's Chortha of the Western Lands. And he aims on being Gatanu—that's why we're here."

"Assignment officer said this was to be police action," Kana returned.

Maybe this was the trouble Mic had sensed back at Secundus. There was a wide difference between policing a turbulent border for a rightful ruler and supporting a rebel chieftain in a bid for a throne.

"Since Skura claims to be the rightful heir, this could be loosely termed police action—"

But Kana thought he detected a dry note in Mills' voice. Had he made a bad error already in uttering a statement which could be taken as a criticism of Yorke's hiring orders?

"Gatanu Plota's sisters were twins. There is some dispute as to who was the elder. Each had a son—so now there's a disagreement over the proper heir. Plota is dying of the shaking sickness—they give him three months more at the most. Skura's party is out of favor at court and Skura was sent here last calm season. He's more an exile than a Chortha. But he made a treaty with Intergalactic Trading for some mining rights and collected enough ready cash to deal with Yorke. The I.T. has been trying to get a foothold here for a long time—the local trade is an iron-tight monopoly of a sort. So they were only too glad to underwrite Skura's bid for the throne. Oh, it's a gamble all right, but if Skura becomes Gatanu he'll pay double what Yorke could collect elsewhere for the same length of service."

"Whom do we fight?"

"S'Tork, the other nephew. He's less of a fire-eater than Skura and has the more conservative nobles and most of the Wind Priests behind him. But he's no fighting man and has no following of troops. Here an army is built around the household warriors of the nobles. And if a lord is not personally popular enough to attract unattached warriors, well, he hasn't an army. Very simple. Skura thinks that with the Horde under his flag it may not even come to battle—that he will be able to bluff the opposition right off the field—"

The pavement ended abruptly at the walls of Tharc and

the wagon trundled on into the ankle-deep dust of a road which was hardly more than a caravan track. They passed under the fangs of a portcullis, out of Skura's capital and into the open country.

A line of guen waited with their merchant owners for open passage into Tharc. Kana noted that these travelers were somewhat shorter than the giant Llor soldiers. Also they were completely muffled in thick hooded robes and stood apart, as silent and featureless as ghosts, to let the Terrans past.

The Horde camp was a mile beyond, the yellow camp lights making a welcome break in the darkness of the moonless night. Under their glow Kana found the tent assigned him, unrolled his bag, and crawled in for a few hours' rest.

There followed a week of intensive drill to shake down the newly assembled Horde into fighting trim—during which Kana was either too occupied with field problems, or too bone tired physically to speculate about his surroundings and the future. But some ten days later they lined up in marching order in the grim gray pre-dawn which on Fronn seemed chillier and more foreboding than the same hour on Terra. The Horde were to move east, toward the distant range of mountains which divided this western province from the rich central plains which the ambitious Skura already thought of as his own.

Kana had to admit that the rebellious Chortha was a perfect example of semi-barbarian war leader. Followed by a troop of fast-riding cavalry, mounted on the hard-to-control male guen, he had pounded through the Combatant camp area on numerous occasions. His popularity with his own people was wide and each day witnessed the arrival of more nobles and their personal retinues to swell the ranks of the native army encamped beyond. Daily, also, the caravans of draft guen wound in to dump supplies or reload material to be transported on to the mountains.

This morning Kana was on point marching duty with Rey, as one such assembly of hooded, muffled drivers and complaining animals shuffled by, raising a thick dust. Once the supply train was on its way, the Horde would swing out too, not on the same trail but across country—with the point men the only contact with the road.

Kana burrowed his chin into the soft lining of his high jacket collar, glad that he had selected one with the fur-lined hood which covered head and ears. The cold of the Fronnian dawn was cruel.

"There goes the last one—" Rey's words came in a puff of milky air as he raised his signal gun and fired a bright red burst into the dark sky.

With rifles resting in the crooks of their arms, the two Terrans fell into the elastic, ground-covering stride of Combatants on march along the edge of the road. Within seconds they caught up to the rearmost gu and were rapidly overtaking the head of the caravan when Kana's attention centered upon one of the robed drivers. He had never seen any of the traders without their figure-concealing garments, but he knew that they were a different race from the hairy Llor who ruled the land.

The Llor cultivated the ground, lived in cities under a loosely feudal government, and were fighters. But these traders, who held a monopoly on both transportation and barter of goods, were another breed. A race nurtured on far sea islands, great mariners and travelers—far roving, but making no permanent settlements on land, they were named Venturi and kept entirely to themselves on the mainland, conducting business only through one of their number in each group who was elected to what they apparently considered the unenviable post of liaison man. The Venturi remained therefore anonymous and ghostly creatures as far as the Terrans were concerned, featureless in their hoods, one exactly like another as to height and gliding walk. Only now—here was one who was different. Where his fellows glided as if they progressed on skates, this one strode. He was not leading a gu either—but journeyed, with empty hands, a little to the right of the regular procession.

Kana's eyes narrowed as he slowed step to keep behind the stranger. It was almost as if this robed wayfarer were not actually one of the Venturi at all. Then Rey drew even with the hooded stray and abruptly the other's pace altered to the gait of his companions. Kana hurried to catch up with Nalassie. They reached the top of a rise. A thicket lay below. The two Swordsmen had either to take to the road to pass it or make a wide detour north. Kana murmured, hardly above a whisper:

"North!"

Rey looked surprised but asked no question. Instead he obediently set a course which would put the thicket between them and the caravan.

"There's a stranger among the Venturi," Kana explained.

Rey slung his rifle and squatted down on the moist turf, detaching a scout's speecher from his belt. "I'll report."

Kana kept on at a steady trot, determined to catch up with the supply train and watch the suspect. He was counting the hooded figures to be sure his man was still among them when Rey joined him.

"Llor cavalry heading toward this road a mile on. If there's anything wrong, they'll handle it. We're to keep out of trouble with the Venturi."

They followed along with the caravan. It was full day now and the sun streaked the sky with yellow. Ahead mounted men milled around some disturbance in the center of the road.

Kana and Rey quickened pace to see what was the matter. A gu was down in the dust, kicking and bearing its formidable fangs at the Llor troopers who were holding consultation over it.

The caravan halted, allowing the Venturi leader to ad-

vance alone. He was met halfway by the commander of
the troop and, after some moments' talk, he returned to
his party for a second conference which led to a second
merchant going on to the stricken gu. The Llor spread out,
leaving only their officers by the animal. Some, Kana
noted, drifted back so that they were now on a line with
the supply train. It must be that they were engaged in
some stratagem—as if they dared not become openly in-
volved in the accusation or search of the Venturi party.

Their trap was sprung with a sudden shout from one of
the troopers. He had dismounted and now his gu jerked its
head loose from his grip on the reins and, blowing a green
foam from its mouth and nostrils, dashed straight for the
beasts of the caravan, its rider running with it, making fu-
tile grabs for the reins.

Before the oncoming fury of the maddened cavalry
mount the heavier-burdened guen went wild, pulling free
from their leading cords, or dragging the Venturi with
them. One of the hooded figures, without any gu, took to
his heels and fled in a pounding run straight for the point
where Kana and Rey stood watching. Kana was tempted
to tackle the fugitive, but the orders had been clear—this
job was to be left to the Llor.

The troopers who were along that side of the road
fanned out and rode to surround the fleeing trader. One of
them whirled over his head a loop of shining stuff which
curled through the air to ring the runner. He changed step,
stumbled when trying to check his speed, and went down
with a crashing force. Some of the Llor dismounted and
walked toward the captive confidently, as if they expected
no further resistance.

But the man on the ground writhed to a sitting position.
And a second later a bolt of red fire struck down the nearest trooper. With a shriek of agony the Llor plunged
across the loose soil.

"Flamer!" Rey yelled.

Both Terran rifles centered and two shots cracked almost as one. The trapped man jerked and fell back to earth with a heavy limpness which told them no more bullets were needed.

A Llor wearing the half circle of an under officer was on the scene, using the butt of his riding bat to roll over a hand weapon of dull metal—one which had no business on Fronn. With that out of reach of the dead hand two of the troopers stripped off the Venturi robe. A Llor lay there, there was no mistaking the curled pelt and the pop eyes of the masquerader.

"This—" The Llor officer touched the flamer with his bat. "Do you know of this?" he spoke slowly in Space Trade Talk.

"It is a firearm—very bad," Kana answered. "We do not use them."

The officer nodded. "Then where get?" he wanted to know, reasonably enough.

Kana shrugged. "This one—he is not of yours?"

The commander of the troop pushed through the ring of his men and bent to stare at the slack face of the native. Then with his own hand he tore away the belt of the fringed kilt. Reversed, the buckle bore an orange-red arrow-shaped mark.

"News-seeker of S'Tork," he identified. Then, lapsing into the native tongue, he gave a series of orders which set the troopers to rolling the body into a torn robe and lashing it on the back of a protesting gu.

To the Terrans' surprise nothing was said to the Venturi. The road was cleared and the supply train plodded on, not one of its guardians turning to look at the group about the spy. The flamer remained in the dust until the commander approached the Combatants and indicated it with the spurred toe of his boot.

"You take—"

It was more an order than a request. But Kana wanted

nothing more than to do just that. This was a problem which must be taken straight to Yorke. What was the latest and most deadly weapon of the Galactic Patrol doing on Fronn in the hands of an enemy spy?

4

CLASSIC MOVE TO DISASTER

On the top of the upturned provision box which served the Blademaster for a table lay the evidence. Fitch Yorke sat on a bed roll, his head and shoulders resting against the knotty trunk of a wind-twisted tree, his blond hair bright against the dark purple-blue of the bole as he chewed reflectively on a stick and regarded the flamer with a brooding frown. But Skura was not inclined to take the matter so quietly.

The Llor rebel leader strode back and forth across the blue clay soil, crushing the calm season ridges in it with grinding boot soles, as if he nursed some spite against the land itself.

"What say you now?" he demanded. "This is not yours. But it is off world. So—then from where?"

"I want to know that also, Highness. This is against our law. But you did not find it in our hands—it was brought by a news-seeker of the enemy."

The "Yaaah" that burst from his woolly throat was more the roar of a hungry feline than an assent. "Evil from S'Tork—could else be expected? Against this—what good are swords—rifles? Are even the weapons of your so-fine Swordsmen strong when they face a fire that cooks and kills? We do not fight with flame. When I take much treasure to Secundus and ask who will give me aid in battle, I am told ask this or that fighting lord—but not such a one, or such a one—for on Fronn only certain ones may fight. So I give up the treasure and you come. Now— S'-Tork numbers among his warriors those who have fire weapons! This is not clean dealing, Terra. And we Llor do not welcome double tongues—"

Skura paused before the flamer and Yorke. "Also"— the woolly head swung around and the pop eyes raked across Kana and Rey—"when the news-seeker was in our hands and could be questioned—what chances? Terran bullets send him speechless into the final shadows. Did you not want him to answer us, Blademaster?"

Yorke did not accept the challenge. "These"—he pointed to the flamer—"are very deadly, Highness. Had not my men killed, none of yours might have lived. I regret that we could not question that spy. Now we can only get our answers from S'Tork's camp—"

"Steps have been taken along that trail. If that refuse from the craw of a byll has indeed such arms we shall know it." Without another word Skura mounted his gu and pounded out of the Terran camp, with his personal guard left several lengths behind as usual, kicking at their mounts with the spur tips of their boots.

When Skura vanished in a cloud of blue dust Hansu and Mills materialized out of the background and Yorke lost his languid pose.

"Well?" One eyebrow slanted inquiringly toward the Blademaster's hairline.

"Better have it out now, rather than later," Hansu returned. "Somebody must be working out of season and with real backing. That's Galactic Patrol stuff—"

"Who?" Yorke spit out a bit of twig.

"Some Mech down on his luck," suggested Mills, "or—"

"Or somebody out to do a little empire building on his

own," Hansu concluded for him. "We won't know until Skura's spies can report back."

"Arms and men—or just arms? That can be pretty important." Yorke got to his feet. "Either way—it's a mess."

Hansu shrugged. "Just arms and *we* have a better chance."

"You think this could be a show-down? Well—could be, could be. But if they think they have us rigged for a smash they'd better revise their plans." The Blademaster did not appear disturbed. "We might even get an answer to the old question too. What if Arch were matched against Mech? On a world such as this the nature of the country would be on our side. A light, highly mobile force against a mechanized division. Strike and away before the heavier body can move—" He looked almost eager to begin such an experiment.

"All right." Hansu picked up the flamer, and his soberness was in contrast to the other's momentary enthusiasm. "Maybe we can have a chance to prove how good we are. But no one can read the future. And this gun gets de-commissioned right now!"

Yorke walked away and then Hansu held his own court of inquiry. Painstakingly Rey and Kana were taken over the events of the past few hours from Kana's noting of the hooded spy to his death.

"Next time see if you can nick a man in a less vital spot," was the Swordtan's comment when they had finished. "I'd give a month's pay to have a few words with that one. Dismissed."

The flamer disappeared and there were no more references to it during the next few days. The Horde was in the foothills of the mountains, winding along paths worn by the clawed feet of the guen. Giant rock ledges layered black and white added to the gloom of the passage. The air, which was rarefied even on the plains, grew more tenuous. And, in spite of their conditioning on the trip to

Fronn, the Combatants were left gasping after each stiff climb. Overhead the sky in daytime held a yellowish tinge and an icy wind licked at them from the snow fields of the peaks.

Seven Fronnian days' travel brought them over the hump and to the down slopes leading to the rich eastern section of the continent. Between the heights and the sea lay only these plains—unless one ventured north to meet another arm of the mountain range.

There had been a few skirmishes with royal outposts. But the three pass forts commanding their road had been abandoned before the rebels reached them, a circumstance which did not relieve Terran minds. Long years of battle training had taught them to be highly suspicious of anything easy. And added to this worry were the rumors that they might just be heading into a trap. The one encounter with the spy had been built into a brush with a group of armed Mechs. And even wilder stories were beginning to make the rounds of the night camps. While Yorke and his officers presented an impassive front, the Combatants kept apart from their native allies—and the service took on the aspect of an engagement from which the off-world fighters would be only too glad to withdraw.

One mid-day Kana accompanied Deke Mills in a tedious climb to the crest of a pinnacle which would afford them a clear view of the road ahead. As Mills adjusted the screw on his far vision lenses, Kana cupped his gloved hands about his eyes and tried his unaided sight. There was a glint below which could only be light striking metal —and it moved.

"They're waiting for us down there," Mills agreed. "Two—three royal standards. Three companies at least. There go Skura's mounted scouts. Wait—they're waving a flag! Parley?"

Kana could just make out those dots drifting down the mountain road to clot in a black blot.

"Yorke should know about this. Tell him they've signaled for a parley and it looks as if Skura is going to oblige—"

Kana slid down to locate the Blademaster at the foot of the pinnacle, occupied with a native map, his three Swordtans in consultation. At the news of the parley Yorke mounted the riding gu Skura had given him and rode off after the native van while Kana climbed back to Mills.

"Look!" The young veteran thrust the glasses into Kana's hand. "Over there—to the left. What do you make of that?"

Kana looked. There was a small body of the Llor rebels riding forward to meet a handful of royalists. But another group had dismounted and were making their way undercover to half circle the conference spot.

"An ambush? But they're meeting under a parley flag!"

"Just so." Deke Mills' voice was dry.

For a long moment there was little action below. The conferring leaders, mounted on guen, remained under the wind-whipped parley standard. Then the hidden rebels struck. The group of officers became a melee of fighting Llor and guen. Rebels dragged unsuspecting royalists from their mounts, leaving some limp upon the ground and pulling others with them back into the shelter of the rocks. As the angry enemy tried to follow, those in ambush covered the kidnappers with a wave of fire from their air rifles until the royalists were forced to retire in confusion. And the parley streamer beat the air over ground occupied only by the dead. The surprise had been as successful as it was treacherous.

The two Terrans, shocked by this drastic betrayal of a code which had been ingrained in them from their earliest days of training, climbed down to join their fellows.

"Something up?" Mic, quick to sense their tension, asked as they scrambled by him.

Kana nodded but Mills did not pause to explain. What that act of violence might mean to the Combatants no one could guess. It might even lead to a complete repudiation of their contract with Skura and their speedy return to Secundus.

Quick as they were about returning to the command post they arrived only seconds before Yorke. The Blademaster's face was an emotionless mask, but the set of his mouth, the gleam in his eyes, showed his worry.

Mills made his report and when he had finished Yorke laughed, though the sound held no mirth. "Yes"—his voice cut across the silence of the group—"it is true, Hansu, Bloor"—he jerked a beckoning finger at the two senior officers—"come along. This is the time for us talk too. And"—his eyes swept the circle of Swordsmen—"you, you, and you—" Kana realized with a start as Mills prodded him in the ribs that he was one the Blademaster had selected, together with Deke and Bogate. A pace or two behind the officers they trotted downhill.

Deke unslung his rifle, a gesture the other two copied. Accurate as the air rifles of the Llor were, the men who used them had neither the skill nor the startling marksmanship of the Terrans. If Yorke needed any show of force to back his meeting with Skura he was going to have it.

They found the rebel leader in a rocky defile where the caravan trail of the mountains widened into a respectable road. Llor mounted and on foot provided an audience for the scene in the center of that dusty track. Three royalist officers, bloody from minor wounds, their arms strapped behind them, were lined up before Skura who was haranguing them in the native language. He paused as the Terrans pushed through the ring of his men. It was impossible for any Combatant to read expression on the furred face of the rebel leader, but it was plain that Skura did not relish the arrival of Yorke.

Together the three Swordsmen planted themselves and their rifles in open view. It might be possible that they would be called upon to use those arms.

Yorke edged his gu on until he was abreast of Skura. The Llor about the leaders pulled back. They had seen too many examples of Terran shooting to wish to provide targets.

"Highness, what have I seen—this is not the proper way of war—" Yorke's voice was not pitched for speech-making but it carried well.

"I am Gatanu, the Gatanu makes war as he pleases," Skura returned. "These serve S'Tork. Men of mine have they killed, so—"

His hand moved in a swift gesture. Steel flashed in the air and the three royalists fell forward as their dark blood splattered as far as Skura's boots.

Yorke's mouth was a single hard line. "That was ill done, Highness. From evil springs evil."

"So? On your world you do as custom rules. Customs are different here, off-worlder!"

The Llor leader was within his rights. And Yorke could make no answer. One of the rules of the Combat forces was not to question any native dealings with each other according to the established customs of the alien world. Perhaps on Fronn the desecration of a parley flag was accepted as a regular move in war time. But Kana heard Bogate mutter:

"No luck outta this—no luck for us when there's blood on a truce flag."

The Blademaster turned and rode away and in a compact group the Terrans fell back to their own force. But added to their constant suspicion was now another disturbing thought. War as they knew it was governed by certain unbreakable rules. Should these few laws to which they had always sworn allegiance be broken, what might be the end?

There was a council of war to which a representative from each team was summoned, while the remainder of the Combatants stood to their arms and prepared for trouble, suspecting attack now not only from the royalists but from their so-called allies as well.

By dawn the decision was made. Since Skura had quoted custom their contract held and under it they must go into battle with the rebels. The royalists had been beaten out of the foothills and the rebel forces were spreading out in long pinchers. Skura had some companies of infantry but guen cavalry was his preferred arm and his few regiments of foot moved as light wings to the heavier Terran Horde. According to his intelligence the royal army opposing them was small. The majority of the great lords of the plains had not yet chosen sides. A quick victory over this force—it was really only the household troops S'Tork had managed to marshal against them— would bring the nobles to declare for the rebels and the whole of the plains would fall to Skura with only a few isolated mopping-up expeditions to be sent against lords stubbornly holding for his cousin.

The shrill fluting of the Llor war trumpets sounded across the rolling country. And the rebels appeared confident of the outcome of the battle as small detachments of foot trotted up to join the wings of the Terran company, and troops of cavalry rode on to establish contact with the enemy.

The Horde stripped for action. Gone were the ornaments and the attention-catching trappings. They were in a uniform green-gray battle dress which blended with the patches of bare soil as they took cover.

Kana stretched his legs along a slight hollow and rested the barrel of his rifle on a conveniently crooked limb of the runty bush which gave him cover. Overhead a flock of flying creatures zigzagged and screeched their fear and anger at this invasion of their private world.

The plan of battle was simple, but one classic in Llor tradition. The pincher claws of the cavalry would attempt to encircle the enemy and herd them in toward the center

where they must face the devastating fire of the Archs.
And since S'Tork's inferior force had been unwise enough
to offer battle the rebels saw no reason why the maneuver
should fail, for the only answer to it was retreat.

Kana looked around as Mills crawled up to join him.
The veteran surveyed the recruit's choice of position criti-
cally before he gave unspoken approval by settling down
to pick his own loop-hole in the cloaking foliage. Under
the blast of the trumpets there was a low rumble of sound,
the deep-throated shouting of the Llor battle slogans. Mills
grinned at Kana.

"The flag's up—here we go!"

Their view of the battle was necessarily limited. And for
what seemed like a very long period of time only the distant growl gave any indication that a struggle was in progress. Then came a burst of riders out of a small coppice.
They milled about, apparently uncertain. But the color of
their trappings was not to be mistaken. These were royalists who had been hunted into the waiting jaws of the trap
in which the Terrans were the teeth.

Another group came out of the wood, and in this several mounts ran free and wild, dodging the men who
strove to catch their reins. A dismounted Llor ran lightly
from cover and behind him hobbled another, using a lance
as a crutch. The hesitating troop which had preceded these
strays broke in two. One, the smaller portion, dressed
ranks, drew swords and rode back into the trees; the
other, keeping very little order, came on down the valley.
Kana picked his target before the fellow came into reason-
able range. Here there were no war trumpets, no battle
songs, but the hidden line of sharpshooters tensed. And, as
the party of fugitives passed that outcrop of rock which
gave the Combatants a range marker, a withering blast of
fire tore them out of their saddles, sending the guen mad
with fear. One or two broken figures crawled along the
ground, but not a rider passed that rock.

Kana could not close his eyes, though his insides

twisted. This proved to be very different from firing at humanoid robots set to dash and dodge across a carefully marked rifle range—which had been his only test of marksmanship before. A second ago he had fired at a good target—that was all the squeeze of the trigger had meant to him then. The Llor he had centered his sights upon had had no identity as a living creature. But—! He gagged and fought against a rising push of nausea. He was given little time to examine his muddled emotion for a second wave of royalists had been beaten out of the wood. This time they were mingled with their pursuers, whirling in a mounted dance of death with a detachment of the rebels who hacked them downslope to the lines of the dead the Terrans had shot. But the enemy were giving a good account of themselves, there were almost as many empty saddles among the rebel band.

"Skura!"

Kana had not needed Mills' identification. The rebel chieftain was unmistakable as he beat and slashed his way to the leader of the loyalist troop. That officer, as imposing physically as the would-be Gatanu, accepted battle with the same eagerness. And, while their followers struggled around them, the two leaders settled down to expert saber work. The royalist was bleeding from a slash high on one shoulder but it did not impair his efficient swordplay. As yet Skura was untouched.

The ring of tempered metal upon metal carried to the Terrans, but they continued to hold their fire. There was too much chance of shooting the wrong man in the melee. The gu ridden by the royalist attempted to use its teeth on Skura's mount. And in one such lunge it jerked its rider out of position. Skura's blade bit deep into the other's forearm and the royalist's sword fell from helpless fingers. Skura had just raised his blade to deliver the death stroke when he himself crumpled, collapsing over his gu's head into the dust.

Perhaps only the Terrans saw that pencil of flame spray

from the wood to strike down the rebel leader in the moment of his triumph. The Llor who, seconds before, had been locked in a death struggle were shocked into quiet, all staring at Skura. Then, with a wild wail of horror and despair, his followers attacked, killing ruthlessly. Two royalists escaped into the woods. The rest were dead.

"That was a flamer!" Kana's voice was swallowed up in the cries of the Llor.

They had gathered up the Chortha's body and were tying it in the saddle. Then they rode north. Mills got to one knee to watch them go.

"That's the end of the war," he remarked.

As if his observation were a signal, the piercing whistle of recall brought the Combatants out of line, withdrawing to secondary positions. Alert and ready the Terrans waited out the afternoon. But what Mills had said at the moment of Skura's fall proved to be true. The death of the rebel chieftain demoralized his followers, the war was at an end and the Llor avoided the off-world men. The Combatants suspected that minor rebels were trying to make deals. And at that moment the future of the Horde was bleak. However, when such defeats had occurred before in Combat history, the Horde or Legion retained by the defeated leader had always been given free access to its transport ships and allowed safe conduct off the planet.

Soldiers are largely conservative, ruled by custom, and since custom was now on their side and they were freed from an entanglement most of them had come to regard as risky, there was a feeling of relaxation, of "Well, the worst is now over," in the Horde camp that night. They kept a patrol about the environs of their position, and there was no slacking on guard. But the death of Skura, who had left no heir to rally his men, absolved them from their pledged support. And now, with something of a holiday lightheartedness, they looked forward to a speedy return to Tharc where the transports waited.

The only gloomy reaction to the events of the afternoon

was the realization that the shortness of the campaign would mean only basic pay. But Kana and some others sensed that the future might not be so bright.

The recruit noted that Yorke, the three Swordtans, and some veterans, including Mills, did not drag out their bed rolls that night. And when he was roused for second guardpost duty in the very early morning he saw the light still shining in the small tent where the officers had gathered.

Skura had been killed with a flamer—which meant that at least one more illegal weapon was in the hands of the enemy. Who had brought the arms to Fronn and why? Kana puzzled over that as he took his post. The chill black of the Fronnian night was alive with sounds which might or might not signal danger. But a circle of guard lamps set at intervals around the camp made a barrier of light.

Flying things attracted there and blinded by the radiance beat around the lamps, making a funnel of winged bodies down to the very lens. Hunting these bemused tidbits came larger creatures, some on four legs and some on two, others skimming on wings themselves. This was rich feasting and not a few vicious quarrels ensued.

Suddenly the low-hanging branches of a bush were pushed aside and a man stepped out into the full beam of the light, halting as if he wanted to be recognized. And the newcomer was no Fronnian.

Kana's rifle went up until its sights covered that swaggering design of crossed rockets on the breast of the stranger's tunic. A Mech—in full uniform! Kana whistled for the guard and snapped:

"Stand where you are—hands up!"

The other laughed. "Not planning to do anything else. I've a message for Yorke."

5

MORNING AFTER

A slap across his sleeping bag shocked Kana into groggy wakefulness some hours later. Mills towered over him.

"Hit dirt," the veteran commanded brusquely. "We're pulling out."

Pulling out they were and with unusual speed. Kana had barely time to throw his bag on a cart already moving. And he was still rubbing the smart of sleep out of his eyes as he fell in with his team. They were marching in "hostile country" order he noticed—scouts out on the wings. And Terran drivers, not Llor, prodded the baggage guen into action. In fact in all that winding column there was not a native Fronnian to be seen. Nor were they headed back into the mountains toward Tharc, but instead following a trail which led away at right angles, north along the foothills.

The new road dwindled into the faintest of tracks within a mile or so. From the exasperated comments voiced about him Kana gathered that none of the lower rank Combatants knew where they were headed or why. And more than once he caught muffled suggestions about the mysterious troubles which had recently overwhelmed other Hordes and Legions light years from home. In spite

60

of their usual fatalism, the morale of the mercenaries might be seriously affected if the situation continued.

Perhaps this new move was the result of that visit the Mech had paid their camp in the early morning. But the confidence the Terrans had shown after Skura was slain was fast changing to a growing uneasiness.

After a space the trace they followed grew so narrow that it seemed they must abandon the carts. Two of the scouts came in to report, a native with them, a Llor of the petty officer class, wearing a stained bandage about his bullet head, one arm in a grimy sling. Rumor rippled down the ranks.

"There's a big river ahead—and no bridge—"

Before that news had reached the tail of the last team the call to general council was whistled. Yorke's voice, clippy and tinny, came through the speakers.

"Men, the situation is not promising. We were informed that S'Tork has enlisted the services of Mech renegades —how many we do not yet know. We have not been offered safe conduct, and we cannot return to Tharc without it. Until we can make a treaty and enforce the recognition of our position under general Combat usage, we must mark time. We shall send a message to Secundus—"

"And who's going to grow a rocket tail and fly it there through space?" Kana heard someone ask grimly in a half whisper.

"We have information," Yorke was continuing, "that there is another mountain gap to the north which we may cross if we cannot come to terms—we are now heading toward that. In the meantime we must do nothing to arouse the enmity of the royalists, give them any reason for declaring that we fought on after the death of Skura. Under no provocation, no matter how severe, is any Swordsman to use his weapons against a Llor—until this order is countermanded. We shall continue in 'hostile country, plan three' until further notice. Change the loads on the large carts to back-packs for the guen. Only the three small handcarts can be used from this point on. We shall establish a night camp beside the river—"

The use of resisting guen for pack animals was not easy. And it was nearly twilight before the detachment of which Kana was one, pulling and batting their snarling beasts down to the lighted area of the camp the van had set up, gained the river. The site of the Terran position was on a bluff above the dark, oily water which washed the clay bank with unwholesome ripples. And an almost vertical descent plunged into a powerful current. They need not fear a surprise attack from that direction.

Kana strode along the bank, looking at the flood. From the white foam collars wreathing the rocks there he judged that the current was too swift to grant them an easy crossing. As his eyes trailed bubbles downstream he saw dancing dots of light moving through the blackness of the night, coalescing on the same bank farther east. Another camp? Then the Horde's line of march must have been paralleled by a detachment of Llor.

Luckily the Horde carried their own rations. Natives who themselves depended upon the natural produce of their land could not readily gauge the superior mobility of an army for whom the supply problem consisted of a relatively small amount of condensed food tablets and other concentrated rations, weeks' needs being carried easily in an individual's own belt pouch. The ancient "scorched-earth" policy would not be effective against Terrans—unless they could be kept from their base for a period comprising months.

"Dumb woolly heads!" As Kana dropped down by Mills and Mic he heard Sim's thick voice rumble, "What do they think they can do—"

"It's not what the fur faces are gonna do." That was Bogate. "Skura wasn't killed by no fur face. I was there. I tell you, fellas, he got burned right through the middle—neat and clean! Me, I'm a Swordsman, and a ten-year man, and I know better'n to spit in the face of a flamer!"

"Flamer?" questioned someone. "But if they had flamers they'd have cut us to pieces back there. And we were winning until Skura took it."

"Lissen." Bogate's voice overbore the other's. "I saw what I saw! That was a Mech that was marched in to see Yorke last night. And he wasn't no observer either! What if S'Tork has a whole renegade Legion hid back there?"

"You're talking feathers and fluff!" challenged one of his companions. "A whole Legion turned bad—why, they couldn't have upped ship for here without Prime knowing it!"

Bogate's sardonic bark of laughter cut that down. "There's a million-trillion ways you can beat the High Brass back at base—and you know it. Just because it ain't never been done before, is no sign that some smart guy can't pull it off. Lookit here, a Mechmaster what wanted to, could grab hisself off a world like this—set up as Control Commissioner or something. Ain't that right, Mills?"

Deke Mills slapped away one of the flyers drawn by the lamps. "Entirely true, Bogate. And you're also right in that exactly that is what may be happening now. If so"— he paused and then continued—"if so we must be prepared to fight our way off-world."

Several voices protested and then sank to silence under Bogate's growl.

"Ain't you bumble-wits got it into your heads yet that when a fella breaks the top laws he ain't gonna let tongues wag if he can help it? We go back to Secundus and shoot off our mouths about flamers and Mechs here and the mop-up crew is gonna head straight to Fronn to see what's what. Think, can't you. Who's liable to have flamers— what kinda support these here renegade Mechs got?"

The sudden tense silence which answered him was that of men who were beginning to think and didn't like it.

Due to Hansu's use of Mills as his aide, Kana's acquaintance with his double was not a deep one. He messed with and shared the quarters of Rey and Mic, meeting with Mills only when duty brought them together. But now he ventured to ask his quiet companion a question.

"This could reach clear to Prime, couldn't it?"

Mills did not turn his head. But a second later he snapped:

"Explain that!"

Kana described the actions of the Mech in the information library, retailing his belief that the man was waiting for the pak on Fronn.

"No Legion badge on his helmet?"

"No, sir. I thought he might have just signed up. But why—" He fell silent but his thoughts were very busy.

How could any Mech be recruited for illegal service on Prime? S'Tork *must* be backed by more than a mere handful of renegades!

"Yes—why and how." Mills' whisper added to his formless apprehension. "This is a case of going into battle blindfolded." The veteran got to his feet and Kana trailed him.

They were, the younger Swordsman discovered, making a circuit of the camp, passing from post to post. When they reached the east Mills gave the password and stepped beyond the brilliance of the lamps into the night. As their eyes adjusted Kana located the bluish haze of the Llor encampment. Contrary to their usual custom the Fronnian forces were keeping their torches ablaze. But they had not advanced any toward the Terran site.

A single moment of study was enough to satisfy Mills. He tramped south, stopping now and then to study the darkness. Farther off was another barrier of lights across the road over which they had just come. The Llor had cut off any possible retreat.

To the west stood the mountain wall. There were no gleams of blue on the heights. The Terran camp was not yet ringed in—or did the Llor believe that the mountains themselves were barrier enough? They might consider that they had the off-world army pinned down with the mountains and the river and the two bodies of their own troops.

Mills reached the last post, but he did not turn back into camp. "Hansu tells me," he began abruptly, "that you're an A-L man. What do you make of the Llor—of this situation? Surely they must know they haven't bottled us up. We could blow them out of our way whenever we wanted to show strength. They have something in reserve —they must have!"

"You can never tell about a feudal civilization with alien natives. Skura was inclined to overestimate his own powers. This is the first time a Combat force has been on Fronn." Kana shrugged. "You know that X-Tee, Alien Liaison, is pure guesswork at times. We can't get inside the skull of a creature whose whole mental processes may be different. The Llor, it's my guess, are either just what they outwardly appear to be—simple barbarians—or else—"

"Or else," Mills caught him up, "something so tortuously complicated that we shall never be able to cope with them. Or they may have expert advice and assistance—"

"From a Mech Legion?"

"I don't see how they could have that! The transportation problem to Fronn alone—! Why, no troopship can clear for anywhere in the Galaxy without a sealed route-tape to its known destination. And yet that Mech on Prime was taking indoctrination for this planet—Prime! Right where the least rumor of such a move should damn it from the start. And suppose a Legion, or a part of a Legion *has* turned rotten—why select Fronn for their operations? What does this frontier world possess that would make such a risk within the bounds of profit?"

"What sort of mineral rights did Skura sell Interplanetary to raise the pay for Yorke, sir?"

Deke Mills squared around to face Kana, amazement in his eyes. Almost, the younger Swordsman thought, as if a gu had addressed him in good Basic.

"Out of the mouths of greenies," he said. "Mineral rights, trading rights, and maybe a good chance for a double cross all around with the Terrans to blame everything on! Lord of Space! That could be the answer to a lot of questions. Mechs could be smuggled in on trade ships—flamers provided—everything! But"—he stared thoughtfully at Kana—"you keep your mouth shut on that bright idea, understand? We already have enough rumors flying around now without adding one so logical it can be believed."

"Then you think we've more than renegades against us, sir?"

"Alien reasoning—how do we know how their minds work? The C.C. doesn't understand, doesn't want to. They've never even tried to know what makes us tick. We're the slightly comical, childish mercenaries—with minds that don't match their pattern charts. So they fit us into the general scheme of things and try to forget us. And because we have functioned in that niche, they've stopped worrying about us. Their idea of a Terran has become so much of a set figure that they do not see us as we are at all, but as they think we are—two very different things. You know"—Mills paused for a moment as if a new thought had struck him—"that in a way gives us a protective covering. We've learned things which would surprise the Galactic Agents. So these Trade boys—non-Terran, of course—Terra cannot trade—figure out a neat, strictly illegal scheme—and they don't stop to think of our part in it at all. We're just pieces to be shoved around on a game board. But what will happen if *we* begin to make moves on our own? We should try just that—"

Kana tensed. Was Mills choosing to pass along real information? Did the Terrans have some way of fighting back against the protective parentalism of C.C. which might even now keep them earthbound? That odd sixth sense which was part of the make-up of any A.L. man quivered into life. He thought of questions—ten—twenty of them—he wanted to ask. But there was no time, for in the camp Swordsmen were moving among the tents and saddled guen stood in the light marking Yorke's headquarters.

"Do we march?" Kana hurried to catch up with Mills.

Before the Blademaster's tent were the three Swordtans and a group of under officers. It was plain there was an argument in progress and at last Yorke turned impatiently from Hansu and reached for the reins of his gu.

"Until I return you're in command," he said.

A party of three Llor, high-ranking nobles by their war harness, were waiting, the lamps painting their furred faces with a slightly sinister shadow. The other two Swordtans mounted, but the Llor leader was in no hurry to leave. He gestured at Hansu and asked a question. Yorke answered, and still the Llor did not move. Yorke's gaze fastened on Mills. He beckoned the young veteran forward. Hansu nodded and snapped the Swordtan's insignia from his helmet, passing it to Deke.

"You're my deputy. The Llor demand that all our High Brass attend. And they've seen you at our conferences in the past so you can pass as an officer. But"—perhaps Kana was the only one who saw that the fingers which passed the badge from one man to the other closed bruisingly tight on Mills' hand—"watch out." Mills mounted a gu and the small cavalcade swept off. Their progress across country was marked by the blue of the Fronnian torches as they sped eastward to the camp of the royalists downriver.

Hansu wasted no time after Yorke left. Working by quiet orders passed from man to man, the Combatants went into action. The tents were left standing. But all other gear was sorted and skeleton packs of one change of clothing, blankets and cold weather wear, were assembled by each man. Medical kits were passed out, along with rations and spare ammunition. Then the men turned in, half a team at a time, for a few hours' sleep. When Kana roused in the early morning the camp presented the appearance of having been sacked by the enemy.

Everywhere the war bags of the Swordsmen gaped, their less useful contents spilled. The force was now prepared to move fast and keep moving. Hansu must expect trouble.

With the rising sun the Terrans could see the hide tents of the royalists on the river bank to the east, and sight the clustered standards of the troops which had followed them through the foothills. The lamps on the barrier were switched off but not dismounted from their bases. For if the Horde had to travel light, these, too, must be left behind.

Hansu had stationed men along the river. Their principal occupation, as Kana observed from an eastern sentry post, was to toss in bits of wood fastened to cords in order to study the current. After about an hour of this they straggled back to report. But Kana knew that to cross the stream here, especially if they were forced into that act under fire, was suicide.

It should not come to that. The Llor had asked to treat. Yorke would return with the safe conduct and the Horde would march back to Tharc. If the Llor followed the rules of Combat that was all they could do—*If*.

Llor rode leisurely down the mountain road, holding their guen to an ambling pace. All wore the royalists' badges, though, as they made a detour about the Terran camp, Kana was not the only one to suspect that the majority had not been on that side of the conflict three days before. They were armed but their weapons were sheathed and slung. And they appeared content to ride slowly to the river, shouting remarks which no Combatant deceived himself into believing were complimentary.

"That woolly-face with the blue sash—" Mic squatted beside Kana in the outpost—"I could make him change his mind about stupid Terrans—with just one squeeze of the trigger—"

The Llor belted with the blue sash was gesturing, gestures which were rankly insulting on any planet. He was escorted by a choice group of friends whose howls of delight led him on to bigger and worse efforts. Mic's sights covered in turn several important points of the comedian's anatomy as he sighted for the shot he could not make.

"Aren't you here ahead of time?" asked Kana.

"Oh, I'm not your relief. We're to double up on the posts from now on, Hansu's orders. There's a nasty smell rising, and it isn't all from wool either. Yorke's been gone almost ten hours. It doesn't take that long to sign a retreat treaty. You bring your pack up with you?"

Kana kicked the roll by his feet. "Sure. But Hansu won't march until he hears from Yorke—"

"I don't think so. Now—just what is that?"

The sun of Fronn was pale and feeble compared to the Sol which warmed Terra, but it did give light and now behind the milling Llor, from the edge of a small thicket on the river bank, those pale rays were reflected by some bright surface directly toward the Terran lines in a regular rhythm.

Three letters of their own native tongue, a cry for aid so old that its origin was long ago lost in the mists of Terra's war-torn past—a signal only one of their own kind would send! Kana laid down his rifle.

"Take over!" He moved before Mic could stop him. His hours of duty at this post had not been wasted. There was a way, if not an easy one, to get down to that coppice without venturing into the open now patrolled by the Llor.

Kana lowered himself over the edge of the cliff, kicking for holds with the toes of his battle boots. Fly-fashion he was able to crawl down to the few inches of beach. There was about a foot of sand and gravel between the base of the cliff and the rushing water. With his back to the wall, hidden from anyone above unless he leaned far enough over to sight him, Kana fought his way by inches along the stream. Once or twice the lapping water curled about his toes and he dug his fingers into the soil at his back for a hold. The worst was losing his sense of distance, for he had to stop every few feet and look up for the trees which were his goal.

How long that crab's journey took he could not have testified, but it seemed to him that he had been at it for at least an hour when the sight of black-green foliage set him turning to face the cliff. A bundle of roots protruded from the bank within reach and he began to climb. Dried clay powdered his face and he wiped his eyes with one hand while he held on with the other. His nails tore and broke and his uniform was plastered with dust and clay, but he wormed his way up into the embrace of a thorny bush.

"Terra?" He kept his voice low. But at the answer to his question he pushed forward recklessly. That moan could only have been born of real suffering.

His forward spring brought him to the very edge of the thicket facing west. Collapsed half over a fallen tree, veiled from the Llor riders by only a thin screen of brush, was a limp body.

Kana hardly dared to touch the body when he saw the extent of the burns which had charred away most of the green-gray tunic. Flamer wound! He shrank from causing the torture he knew his grip must bring as with infinite horror he raised the other. The blackened, seared body writhed out of his hold and a moan sounded the wounded man's pain. Gritting his teeth, Kana took hold for the second time and fought the other's feeble attempts to pull free. At last he turned the heavy head to the light. The flamer had not touched the face and though it was contorted and twisted with agony, Kana knew who it was he supported in his arms.

"Deke! What—what have they done!"

6

IF THE FAITH HE BROKE—

The dark eyes struggled to focus. It was as if Deke Mills came haltingly back from a long distance, driven by some overwhelming sense of duty.

"All—dead— Hart Device— Tell Hansu—Hart Device—"

Kana nodded. "I should tell Hansu that Hart Device is responsible?"

Deke's eyes gave assent. "No—not alone. Galactic—agent—hiding— Burned us down." Some spark of strength steadied his voice. "Tried—tried to get Yorke to renegade too. When he said no—flamed us from behind. All dead—thought me dead too. Agent came—looked. I saw him clear—agent—tell Hansu—C.C. backing Device. Crawled —crawled—hours and hours crawled. They had just flamers—no big stuff. Tell Hansu—flamers—"

"There's a Galactic Agent with them and they have C.C. arms," Kana repeated with cold steadiness.

For a long moment Mills lay quiet in his hold, summoning up strength.

"Tell Hansu—C.C. behind it—wipe us out if they can. Mustn't be cut off here. Back to ships—report—Combat —report—"

One of the charred stumps of hands stirred, pawed at Kana's sleeve.

"I'll tell him, Deke," he hastened to promise.

"From behind—no chance—Hart Device—" Mills' whisper thinned and then died. Then he said quite clearly and coherently:

"Give Grace, Comrade—!"

Kana swallowed, his mouth dry. For an instant he was back again in the chapel on Terra, half the Galaxy away from this Fronnian wood. He had been drilled in the Ritual, he knew what had to be done. But somehow, in spite of all the solemn instructions, he had never really expected to be called upon to give the Last Grace—

Deke's pain-filled eyes held his. His duty done, he was waiting for the release from the world of agony which held him. Mills knew what his wounds meant. Nothing could be done for him even by the Medicos on Secundus. And he could not be transported there. Slowly, trying not to add to Mills' pain, Kana lowered the other to earth and opened his own tunic to reach the slender knife all Combatants wore on their breasts. This was the "Grace" of the fighting man—to be carried with him awake or sleeping all his life—to be used for one purpose only.

Kana drew the steel into the light. He raised the plain cross hilt to his lips and said the proper words, hearing his own voice as if it belonged to a stranger, knowing that Deke's twisted lips were trying to shape the same plea.

"—so do I send thee home, brother-in-arms!" Kana ended, he could not delay any longer.

The knife slipped into the place instruction had taught him to seek. Then he was alone—left to slip that wet blade back in its sheath. It could not be cleaned except in the earth of Terra. There was one thing more—the husk which had been Deke Mills must not be left for the Llor and it was beyond his power to carry the body back to camp.

From his belt Kana unhooked a cartridge. With great

care he unscrewed its cap and placed it on the body. Then he threw himself back toward the cliff. The blast came in a sheet of flame before he was quite over the bank. When that fire died Deke Mills would never be found.

Kana inched his way upstream at the fastest pace he could manage, trying to keep his mind blank of all but Mills' message to Hansu. With Yorke and the other Swordtans murdered, Trig Hansu now commanded the Horde.

He found the end of a rope dangling over the bluff below the sentry post and with its aid got up to the camp. At the top he found not only Mic but Hansu waiting for him. Downriver a pillar of black smoke penciled into the sky and the Llor were gathering at the edge of the wood. Kana made his terse report.

"They flamed Yorke and the rest from behind when Yorke would not agree to join them. A C.C. Agent watched the whole thing secretly. Hart Device leads the Mechs. Deke was mortally wounded but crawled—as far as the wood over there. He said he saw C.C. flamers but none of their big stuff—thought that they were out to get us all."

Hansu's expression did not change at the name of the renegade Mechmaster or at the mention of the Agent. And almost before Kana finished speaking he was giving orders to the handful of veterans nearby.

"Dolph, you take over Team One, Horvath, Team Two. Prepare to move out. And send Bogate here."

Hansu asked one more question of Kana in a low voice: "Mills?"

Kana found no words to answer that. He drew out the Grace Knife to display its stains. Behind him, through his sick misery, he heard Mic's breath catch. But Hansu made no comment. And he asked nothing more.

It was Mic who helped Kana sling his rifle and shoulder his pack, guiding him back to the busy camp. The gear they had discarded the night before was being built, under Bogate's orders, into a wall of supplies stretching from one lamp line to another. Except for the men working to erect that barrier the Combatants were lining up to the west, facing the mountains.

"Done, sir!" Bogate saluted Hansu. Five of the Terrans were stationed at intervals along the discarded baggage, and each cradled in his hand one of the fire cartridges.

"Ready with those beasts?" demanded Hansu.

The squad which had herded the pack guen to the far side of the camp shouted an affirmative.

"Men"—Hansu wheeled to face the teams—"you all know what has happened. If the faith be broke, then so is the contract which bound us. Yorke and the others were murdered, shot down from behind by flamers. Mills lived long enough to warn us. You know that it is not superior numbers, or strength of arms, that wins a war. The side which goes in with the will to victory has the advantage. When we march out of here we have to cross a hostile planet. Every native may be ranged against us. But unless we can reach Tharc we have very little chance. Remember this—our lives are at stake, yes. But the Combatant whose single aim is to keep alive usually dies in the first charge. To die is our common lot, no man escapes that. But if we die in the tradition of the Hordes—that is a good ending for any of us.

"They believe that they have us walled in, that we cannot break out of their cage of mountains, river and troops. But we shall show them that they dare not underestimate a Swordsman. With this fire to cover our tracks we shall head west—into the mountains. Before the death of Skura they told us that the mountains were to be feared, that the natives there have never submitted to the Gatanu's rule and are dangerous. If that is so we may find allies—at least we shall be headed in the right direction. Whoever wants to keep alive must aim at victory. It is the winners who kill and the losers who are killed!"

The Horde greeted that statement with a cheer as Hansu

signaled the men by the barrier. Squalling guen were sent running wild toward the Llor who milled around beyond the boundaries of the camp. And the Fronnian troopers were forced to scatter before the loose animals, trying to head them away from their own lines. But the guen, with the diabolical tempers of their kind, attacked the cavalry mounts wherever they came in contact.

Falling into "hostile country" order the Horde moved out. Puffs of flame blossomed along the wall of abandoned supplies, providing a thick smoke to hide their going. And the heat of the fire would keep back the Llor for some time.

The Terran line of march followed the river where there was little cover. And within half a mile the stream sank deeper as outcrops of black and white rock grew more frequent. Kana took his turn at hauling the small carts which transported such of the general supplies as they had to have. There were two of these and the material they carried might mean the difference between life and death for the men they rolled among.

It was close to twilight when Kana released his hold to a relief and, rubbing his rope-chafed hands, fell back into line. So far Hansu had given no orders to camp. They ate as they marched, hard rations, and sipped the water from their canteens. There had been no signs of pursuit. But the Blademaster evidently intended to put as many miles between them and their last camp as was humanly possible.

The river stopped them for the second time. Sunk now in a deep gorge, it sliced across their route. They would either have to cross or turn back. In the last dwindling light of day they made camp, taking advantage of the rough ground to conceal their bed rolls. It was then that Kana was summoned to report to Hansu.

"You were down to the stream edge back there. Current bad?"

"Slick and fast, sir. And I think deep too. It must be even deeper here."

"Hmm—" Hansu dropped to his knees and wriggled forward to the rim of the drop. He brought out a pocket flash and lowered it by a cord into the depths, revealing the surface of the cliff as it descended.

The river had cut that gorge, and at times it must have been a wider and stronger stream, for it left in its passage a series of ledges—a giant's staircase, marking the stages of its sinking. Not very wide and unfortunately far apart— they were still ledges and so promised a means of winning down to the water. The light oscillated above the racing flood and the vicious fangs of boulders made up rapids which choked half its bed. Landslides had partially dammed the stream, leaving a residue in stones too big for the water to tear away. To try to swim that would be asking for a smashed and broken body. And the light's rays were too limited to show what awaited on the other side. Hansu coiled the rope, loop by loop, bringing up the light.

"We'll have to wait for daylight," he said impatiently. "A Galactic Agent—you are sure Mills said that?"

Kana could only repeat what he had been told. Then he added: "The Llor are confident, sir—a lot too confident. Wouldn't they have to be pretty sure of their backing before they turned on us?"

Hansu made a sound which had little in common with real laughter. "Oh, yes, we have reputations. But then they must have advisers to whom such reputations are merely amusing. The Llor are fighting men and if the advantages appear to lie on their side, they are going to do just as they please. Skura murdered his enemies even under the parley flag, this will be more of the same. Maybe it's all an old Fronnian custom. However"—his lips drew back in what was close to a lion's snarl—"they had better not make too many bright plans for the future —even acting under C.C. advice!"

"What do you know about the Cos?" the Blademaster

demanded a moment later, snapping Kana out of some dark thoughts.

"They are mountain natives, aren't they, sir? There wasn't much about them in the pak on Fronn. I got the impression that they're not of the same race as the Llor and that they are deadly enemies of the plains dwellers. But they aren't Venturi either."

"They're a pygmy race—at least the Llor consider them so. And they *are* deadly—to anyone who tries to invade their territory. Use poison darts and mantraps. But whether we're headed into Cos country now, I don't know. And their quarrel may be only with the Llor—there's always that hope. Anyway, we have no choice but to advance. And now you're going to work, Karr."

"Yes, sir?"

"You're attached as Alien Liaison man from now on. Figure out what you need for a 'first contact pack' and get it together tonight. We'll have no time in the morning and you must have the kit ready to use. Bogate!"

The veteran, a black blot in the deepening night, moved up.

"You take scout tomorrow. Karr here will be the AL man for your party."

"Yes, sir." There was no indication that Zapan Bogate had ever seen Kana before. "How many men?"

"Not more than ten. Wide scout—hostile country. I want a con job all the way—"

"Yes, sir! Con it is!"

The feeble illumination in the camp came from hand flashes muffled in spider silk. But it was enough to guide Kana to his place with Mic and Rey. He hunched down, drawing his one blanket about his shoulders, and tried to think coherently. As AL man with the advance scouts tomorrow he would have to have some kind of a trade kit —trade was always the easiest form of contact with unknown tribes. But he knew so little about the Cos—pygmies, perpetual enemies of the Llor, addicted to poison darts and mantraps to keep their mountain territory sacrosanct. The common offerings—food—adornment. This problem should have been foreseen before they burned the excess baggage. If the Combatants had obeyed orders they had already stripped themselves of the very things he would need.

Food— Almost all aliens had an innate curiosity about off-world food, especially if they lived in a rugged country on a near to starvation diet. And of all Terran foods there was one in particular which the Combatants always carried with them, one grown only on their native world, which most extraterrestrial life relished. Intersystem Traders had been trying to export it for years. But the Terrans had ruled it a military supply and so controlled its production—keeping it for the troops and a few of their favored alien friends. As a bargaining point it had been too precious to destroy back at the last camp. Their ration of it must be lashed on one of the carts he had helped to drag. He should ask the Medico for a supply.

Ornaments—the veterans had stripped their wealth from the dress uniforms. Each man would carry his own in a waist treasure belt. Kana must beg for the showiest pieces. Well, no time to lose. Neither Mic nor Rey owned anything worthwhile. But there was the whole camp to canvass.

Kana dropped his blanket wearily and started off on his task, his first quarry being the Medico. Crawfur heard his plea and then detached one of the small boxes from the nearest cart. Kana signed for a packet as big as his hand —a packet which would have brought the equivalent of a deputy-control officer's pay for half a year had it been offered for sale in the black markets on half a dozen different planets.

And on hearing of the other need Crawfur unhooked one of the pockets of his own belt and contributed to the cause a Sirius "Sunstone" which drew light from a muffled lamp to make a warm pool of fire in the donor's hand.

"Might as well take this. My neck's worth more than that. Don't hesitate to ask—we all know what we may be up against. Tal, Kankon, Panoy." He roused his assistants and explained.

When Kana left the group he had the packet of sugar, the sunstone, a chain of Terran gold about a foot long, a ring made in the form of a Zacathan water snake, and a tiny orb of crystal in which swam a weird replica of a Pothaian fish-lobster. He returned to his own place half an hour later the breast of his tunic bulging with glittering treasure, rings on every finger and arm bands braceleting his arms. The loot was sorted out under a lamp. This and this and this were eye-catching, "come-on" pieces to be displayed as a lure. But this and that and that should be reserved as personal gifts to win the favor of chieftains or war leaders. He made up three packets according to their future use and put them away before he curled up and tried to sleep. Without the bright rim of the lamps about the campsite the heavy dark of the Fronnian night walled them in—they might be within a giant box trap, the lid slammed down upon them.

Kana could see those icy sparks of light which were the stars—suns which warmed strange worlds. And somewhere, overshadowed by the brilliance of so many others, Sol had its place, while around its yellow glory wound in their orbits the worlds he knew best.

Green earth. Out here there were other green worlds, as well as blue, red, white, violet, yellow—but none of them wore just the same tint of green as that which covered Terra's hills. Terra—man's home. Mankind had come late into space, and had been pushed to one side of the game Central Control managed. But there were many worlds where native life had never reached intelligence. What if man had been allowed to spread to those—to colonize? What if the very ancient legends of his race were true and there had been earlier trips into deep space from which the voyagers had never returned? Were there worlds

where once Terran colonies had taken root? Where he
could find his own distant kin free of the Central Control
yoke, men who had won the stars by their own efforts?

He drifted into sleep thinking of that. But then he was
crouched in a Fronnian thicket, a bloody knife in his
hand—

"—up!" Kana rolled over. The dawn was gray and
above him Bogate, rifle slung over his shoulder, marching
supplies in place, stood, his thumbs hooked in his waist
belt, his helmet gleaming in the growing light.

Kana rolled his own kit together hurriedly. The AL
packets he crowded into the front of his tunic where he
could reach them easily.

"Moving out now?"

"Shortly. Draw your rations and fall in."

Hansu and a picked party equipped with ropes were already busy at the rim of the canyon. Three men had
worked their way, ledge by ledge, to the sliver of beach far
below. There they took turns, one roped to another, wad-
ing and swimming out into the flood, wedging native
lances and driftwood between the boulders, trying to make
a barrier which might save a man, swept from his feet,
from being washed away. It was plain that Hansu was determined to get them across the river.

The pioneers below had fought their way less than half
the distance across when Kana, together with Bogate's
scouts, started down. They fastened rifles, packs, and
other supplies into waterproof coverings which were lowered on a makeshift platform faster than they climbed.
Kana was dangling on a rope between two ledges when a
shout which was half scream tore at his ears and nerves.
He did not turn his head—he dared not. A moment later
the rope a few feet to his right, taut seconds before with
the weight of the scout who had crawled over the rim beside him, slapped the rock loosely—that weight gone.

Even when his boots rested on the next ledge Kana did not look down. He rested, spread-eagled against the wall, his fingers gritting on the rock, the sweat dripping from his chin.

Three ledges more and he reached the shingle. The men who had preceded him were still gazing downstream, a bewildered horror in their eyes. But there was no time to mourn as there had been none to save. Bogate slid down the last length of rope and was shouting orders:

"Get your gear, you Lothurian leaf eaters! We cross over and then we go up—and we do it in space time!"

They did it—if not in space time—with the loss of another man, sucked under by the current and smashed against a rock, then by some freak of the flood flung contemptuously back at them limp and broken. But roped, sometimes thrown off their feet and carried downstream, fighting from one boulder to the next, they got across. Another of their company, nursing an arm snapped like a twig during his final two-foot fight for the shore, remained there to watch the guide ropes they had left for those following.

Up the cliff they crept from handhold to handhold, shaking with effort, their fingers slippery with sweat, their hearts and lungs laboring. Salt stung in their eyes and the rawness of their hands, but they climbed.

Kana concentrated on the foot of earth immediately before his eyes, and then on the next higher and the next. This had gone on for hours—would go on and on without end.

Then a hand closed about the wrist he had extended for a fresh hold and he was lifted with a yank which brought him sliding on his face across the lip of the wall to lie panting in tearing gasps, too bone weary to reach for the canteen which held the water his mouth and throat craved.

He sat up as Bogate came along. There was a coil of

rope about his waist—that must be knotted to other lengths, the whole dropped to form a ladder for the Horde.

Kana drank and was able to scramble to his feet when their rifles and packs were hoisted. Nor was he the last to fall in as Bogate gave the signal to move on—into the dark future of the mountains.

7

THE BADLANDS

As they left the river the rest of the scouts fanned out. Only Kana continued with Bogate. He was a supernumerary in this operation, his duties beginning if and when they found traces of intelligent life. To his surprise, instead of ignoring his presence entirely, Bogate waited for him to catch up, asking:

"Just what do we look for?"

"Hansu thinks we may find Cos—they're a pygmy race supposed to inhabit these mountains—hate the Llor and are highly dangerous—use poison darts and build man-traps."

Bogate's reply to the sketchy information was a grunt. The wind was rising in gusts which whistled eerily between the heights, propelling the migrating puff-balls—circular masses of spiky vines which traveled so until they found water where they could root for a season. Of a sickly, bleached, yellow-green, they were armed with six-inch thorns and the Terrans granted them the right of way. This was the start of the Fronnian windy season. And to fight across the ranges during that period was to front dangers no Llor would willingly face.

A weird moaning rose to a shriek among the rocks far

above them as the wind was forced through crevices and cracks. But for the most part the scouts were sheltered from the full blast by the ridges.

Here the soil was a mixture of gravel and clay, liberally salted with the rocky debris of slides. Each side canyon or gully had to be blazed with a fluorescent brand so that the Horde would keep to the main trail. They detoured about boulders taller than a man until Kana began to wonder why such a large number of landslides should occur in the length of a single dried watercourse. Suddenly the answer to that lay before his eyes and it was grim.

Sun flashes reflected from something half buried in the soil. He knelt to scrape away the earth. A Llor sword protruded from under a rock. And its haft was still encircled by the finger bones of a skeleton hand!

"Smashed flat—like a bug!" was Bogate's comment. The veteran's eyes narrowed as he looked along the way they had come and then on up the slit at the dusky shapes of the mountains. He had been too well trained to outré forms of warfare on half a hundred planets not to mistake clues.

"Rolled rocks and caught 'em. Neat. This Cos work?"

"Might be," Kana assented. "But it was a long time ago—" He was interrupted by a shout which sent Bogate sprinting ahead.

The narrow canyon they had chosen to follow widened out into an arena—an arena where a deadly game had once been played and lost. Bones brittle with years carpeted the arid floor. And Llor skulls, very human looking, mingled with the narrow, fanged ones of guen, were easy to identify in the general litter, but not one skeleton was unbroken or entire. Kana picked up a rib, the bone light in his fingers. He had been right—those deep indentations could only be the marks of crushing molars. First there had been a killing and then—a feasting! He pitched the bone away.

Keeping aloof from the mass of ghastly relics the Terrans walked around the wall of the valley. There were no weapons in that gray waste, no remains of Llor war harness. Even the trappings of the guen were missing. The dead had been stripped completely. And since they lay unburied, the massacre must have gone unavenged.

"How long ago, d'you think?" Bogate's throaty bellow was subdued.

"Maybe ten years, maybe a hundred," Kana returned. "You'd have to know Fronnian climate to be sure."

"They got caught bunched," Bogate observed. "Larsen," he snapped at the nearest scout, "climb up and use the lenses—cover us from above from now on. I'll take point on the other wall. The rest of you—go slow. Soong, report back on the speecher. We haven't seen nothin' livin' so far. But we don't want *our* fellas caught like this!"

At a snail's pace they progressed to the far end of the valley of death, threading the narrow opening there as if they feared any second to hear the roar of an avalanche. But Kana, taking notice of the barren countryside, thought that the Cos would not ordinarily inhabit that section. The slaughter behind them might be the sign of some war—if Cos *had* caused that havoc. The tooth marks on the rib continued to haunt him. Some primitive peoples ate enemy dead, believing that the virtue of a brave foe could be so absorbed by his slayer. But surely those scars on the bone had never been left by the molars of a humanoid race!

There were other meat eaters in plenty on Fronn. The ttsor, large felines, the hork, a bird or highly evolved insect (the record-pak had not been certain) a smaller species of which was tamed and used by the nobles of the land for hunting, much as the ancient lords of his own world had once flown their falcons for sport. Then there were the deeter, concerning the exact nature of which no one could be certain for they were nocturnal and dug pits to trap their prey. But those mysterious creatures inhabited the swamp jungles of the southern continent. Which left—the byll! But he had thought that those highly dangerous, huge, flightless birds were only to be found on the plains where their speed in the chase earned them their food. More dangerous than the ttsor—who did not willingly attack—the bylls were twelve feet of bone, muscle, wicked temper and vicious appetite.

This mountain country was bare of vegetation except for a few clumps of knife-edged grass, withered and sear from the long dryness of the calm season. On the plains this grass was ruthlessly burnt off by the Llor, but in these mountain gullies it flourished in ragged patches to slash the skin of the unwary.

The scouts took hourly breaks, ate ration tablets, drank sparingly from their canteens and pushed on. The rugged country about them might be a lunar landscape in their own system, lacking all life. It was when the dried stream bed they followed branched into two that Bogate called a halt. Both of the new canyons looked equally promising, though one angled south and the other north. The Terrans, shivering a little in the bite of the wind from the snow peaks, were undecided.

Bogate consulted his watch and then compared its reading with the length of the shadows beyond the rocks.

"Quarter of an hour. We split—return here at the end of that time. You"—he indicated four of the scouts— "come with me. Larsen, you take the rest south."

Kana scrambled up the wall of the northern fork, lenses slung around his neck. Zapan Bogate was in the lead and had gained on his companions. The man immediately below Kana was having heavy going. Slides blocked his assigned route and he had to make frequent detours.

It was by sheer chance that Kana caught that flicker of movement behind Wu Soong. A rock shadow bulged oddly. He swung his rifle and shouted a warning. Soong threw himself flat behind a rock and so saved his life. For the ugly death which had been stalking him struck—empty air.

Kana fired, hoping to hit some vital spot in that darting red body. But the thing moved with unholy speed, its long scaled neck twisting with reptilian sinuosity. He was almost certain he had hit it at least twice but its frenzied darts at the rock where Soong had gone to earth did not slow. No longer silent, it shrieked its furious rage with a siren blast which tore their ears.

A burst of white fire enveloped the byll. When that cleared the giant bird lay on the ground, headless but still struggling to move its shattered legs.

"Bogate," Kana shouted down, "those things sometimes hunt in packs—"

"Yeah? Fire the recall, Harv," he ordered one of the awe-stricken men. "That ought to bring Larsen. We'll stick together. If there's any more of them, stalkin' us in crowds, we're gonna be ready for 'em. And not all scattered out so close to dark."

Soong made a wide circle around the body of the byll to join the others as Bogate gave Kana an order.

"You keep an eye out—cover us back to the forks."

From then on they investigated every shadow, every crevice in the canyon walls. It was with a sigh of relief Kana saw them back to the fork where Larsen and his men waited. Bogate put them all to work at once, rolling up good-sized boulders, erecting a breastwork which should stop any byll's charge.

"Those things hunt at night?" he wanted to know.

"I don't know. By rights that one shouldn't have been back here in the mountains at all. They're meat eaters and their regular territory is the central plains."

"Meaning that if they do come here, it's because they *can* hunt?"

Kana could only nod in agreement. As arid as the country seemed to be, it must harbor life—enough life to attract the bylls.

Since a fire was out of the question—they dared show

no lights—the scouts huddled together behind the wall of their temporary fort. The mountains cut off the light of the sinking sun and in the gloom Kana found himself listening —for what he did not know.

The wind rose again to swoop and wail. But through their hours of travel the Terrans had become so accustomed to its moans that they no longer heeded it. In one of the infrequent intervals of quiet, when the mountain blasts died, Kana listened again. Had he heard—? But nothing stirred beyond the wall.

They slept in fitful snatches, two of their number on watch in turn. Kana was dreaming when an elbow in his ribs brought him into full wakefulness and Soong's sibilant whisper warmed his ear.

"Look!"

Up and far ahead was a wink of light—a light which flickered to prove that it was no star. And to its left—another! Kana used the lenses. Those were fires right enough —beacons! In all he counted five. And beacons on those heights could only mean that someone was alert to the Terran invasion of this mountain territory. Not the royalists—the flames were not the blue of Llor torches. As he watched one winked and disappeared, then it blinked out again—off and on—in a pattern. There was no mistaking the meaning of that—signals! Would that exchange of information lead to such a one-sided battle as had taken place in the arena they had crossed that day?

"Signals!" Bogate was awake and watching also. "They must have spotted us!"

Kana heard rather than saw the veteran scramble over the wall. A moment later a growl from the dark relayed the other's displeasure. Kana climbed the barrier to look back along the route they had come. He saw then what had brought that grunt out of Bogate. High on the cliffs which walled the canyon was a speck of light. But they had no more than sighted it than it disappeared, not to be sseen again. An answer to the signal ahead?

The veteran cleared his throat with a rasp. "Maybe that was 'orders received.' " He parroted the official phrase. "Soong, use the speecher. Tell Hansu about those signals—"

"Well," he added a few moments later, "the show must be over for tonight—"

He was right, three of the fires ahead were gone, and the two remaining seemed to be dying. Kana shivered as icy fingers of wind pried within his coat. Were they going to walk into trouble?

"Camp answered," Soong reported out of the dark. "They saw a fire a little ahead of them, but not the others. Told 'em about the byll, too. They're at this end of the bone valley."

"Good enough. Turn in. We'll go on tomorrow."

In the morning Bogate chose the southern fork of the old river for exploration. Since Tharc lay to the south, it was logical to head in that direction. Whether the presence of byll in the other valley influenced his decision, or the fact that the fires they had watched had been to the north were points he did not discuss with the rest of the scouts.

Their new path was clearer of rock slides than any they had found so far and within a half mile Kana noticed an upward slope. They were climbing at last, instead of burrowing at the bottom of rock-walled slashes.

But they had not been an hour on their way before they came upon their first trace of the mountaineers. Luckily their experience with the byll had made them overly cautious and they were constantly alert to any faint indication of the abnormal. Larsen, who was in the lead, stopped abruptly at the edge of a wide, smooth expanse of sand. When Bogate came up the scout pointed to a curious depression in the center of the strip.

Kana, recalling one of Hansu's warnings about the Cos, spoke first:

"Might be a trap—"

Bogate looked from the recruit to the depression. Then

he walked away to choose a stone, under the weight of which he staggered, waddling up to plump his burden onto that smooth surface.

There was a crack. Sand and stone together rushed down into a gaping hole. Kana inched up to look. What he saw made his insides twist as his imagination leaped into action. It was a trap, all right, a vicious, deadly trap. And the captive who fell into it would die a lingering, tortured death on the spikes artfully planted below.

The Terrans exchanged few words as they crept around the edge of the pit. On the other side Soong reported on the speecher, informing the Horde of this new risk.

From then on their progress slowed to a crawl. Not only must they watch for bylls, but every smooth patch of ground underfoot became suspect. They tested three more such stretches by Bogate's method, to have the last open again into darkness, this time a darkness from which such a frightful stench arose that they made no attempt to examine it closer.

"Do we now journey straight to someone's front door?" Soong shifted the weight of the speecher from one hip to the other.

"If we do—he's the sort who doesn't welcome visitors." Kana's attention was divided between the cliffs which walled in the stream bed and its flooring—death might come suddenly from either direction. And *he* was the AL man—the one supposed to contact the opposition. But none of the training he had known prepared him for a situation such as this—bare mountains which showed no signs of life—and these unmanned defenses against invaders. You couldn't contact an enemy who wasn't there. The Cos—if Cos they were—plainly pinned their faith on the devices of the weak or few in number—devices which would kill at a distance without involving too closely those who used them. If he could only bring about a meeting, convey to the mountaineers the idea that the Horde, winding its way into their jealously guarded territory, had no quarrel with them—on the contrary was now arrayed against their own ancient enemy, the Llor!

He was reasonably sure that any Cos spying on them would be stationed on the heights. And when the scouts took their break at the end of an hour's advance, he approached Bogate with a plan of his own. The veteran surveyed the tops of the cliffs uneasily.

"I dunno—" He hesitated. "Yeah, if they're spyin' they're up there—I'll grant you that. But they may be miles away—and we can't lie around waitin' for you to prowl, huntin' for somethin' which maybe ain't there. We'll see later—"

Kana had to content himself with that half promise. But the country offered an argument on his behalf not many minutes later. They rounded a curve and found themselves fronted with a wall of rock down which the vanished river must once have crashed in a spectacular falls. Bogate waved to Kana.

"Well, here's a place where somebody's gotta climb. Suppose you do it and see what you find. Take Soong with you."

They shucked off their packs, taking only their rifles, and began the ascent—not up the water-worn face of the falls but along the relatively rough cliff to the left. After he finished this enlistment, Kana thought as he crept fly-wise from handhold to handhold, he would be qualified for service with a crack mountaineering Horde.

When they reached the top they faced west gain. Here once more was the bed of the stream, but it was narrower than in the canyon below. And not too far ahead the native somberness of the rock was broken by patches of yellow-green vegetation which promised moisture.

"There is something—" Soong pivoted slowly, studying the landscape.

Kana sensed what bothered his companion. He, too, felt as if they were under observation. Together they surveyed every foot of the rocky terrain. Nothing moved and the wind tore at them, whirling dust devils before it over the edge of the falls. They were alone in a dead world—and yet something watched! Kana knew it by a twitching between his shoulder blades, a cold crawling which roughened his skin with nervous tension. They were being watched—with a detached, non-human curiosity.

"Where is it?" Soong's voice came plaintively between the howls of the wind.

Kana knelt in the sand and brought out his number one package for trade contact. He selected a bare stretch of stone and laid out upon it the pieces he believed flashy enough to catch the eye and pin the attention of any native. Then he pulled Soong with him to the far left, picking out concealment well above the stream bed.

As the minutes passed Kana began to wonder if his nerves had misled him. The gold chain, the handful of bright stones drew the weak sunlight to make a flashing pool of fire which would have attracted the attention of any watcher, would have brought him out of cover had he been of any race the Terrans knew.

"Lord of Space!" Soong's voice hissed between his teeth.

Something had moved at last. A shadow floated with liquid, feline grace between two rocks and stood above the trade station. Kana's breath caught. A ttsor! That greenish fur—treasured by the Llor for mantles of state—could not be mistaken. The round skull with its large brain case, the fringed ears— A tail, able to grasp and hold, whipped around and selected the length of gold chain from the display, holding it up before the large yellow eyes. The ttsor sniffed at the rest of the collection, using the giant thumb claw of one paw to spread them around, and dropped the chain. It was not interested in what had no food value.

Kana's hand shot out to depress the barrel of Soong's rifle.

"It won't attack—don't shoot!"

The ttsor stiffened, its body tense, its head pointed upstream. Then in an eye wink it was gone and they saw it speeding away, up out of the river bed to the heights.

A sound reached them above the moan of the wind—a muffled roar Kana could not identify. He looked upstream. Then he whirled and grabbed for Soong, dragging him back from the lower part of the valley which was now a deadly trap. Together they ran for the cliff. Kana saw the white faces of those below turned up to him. Soong fired into the air—the three spaced warning signals—and Kana waved his arms trying to urge the others back against the canyon walls. His message must have made sense for they scattered and ran—some to one side and a few to the other. How many made it he did not have a chance to see before the black wall of water poured over the lip of the falls to hide the scene in a wild welter of spray.

The flood arose to lap at Kana's boots, lashed at him with spray. Shoulder to shoulder with Soong he wedged himself between anchoring rocks. Again the unseen mountaineers had used nature to defend their country, had turned loose this flood to rid their land of invaders. Soong was busy with the speecher trying to warn the Horde marching along the path of disaster.

8

DEATH BY THE WATER—
DEATH BY FIRE

Out of the foam below broke the head and shoulders of a man fighting his way to safety, tugging a weaker struggler behind. They groped to the air and clung, braced against boulders, as the waters dashed over them. And across the canyon Kana thought he saw another dark figure reach safety. Did only three survive?

With Soong he angled down the wall and helped drag Bogate and the half-conscious Larsen out of the grip of the flood. Shivering, the four wedged themselves on a narrow ledge, only a foot or so above the stream which showed no signs of shrinking. Bogate shook his head, as if to clear away some mist as tangible as the spray still drenching them.

"Somebody musta pulled a cork," Larsen commented between coughs.

"D'you see anything up there?" Bogate wanted to know.

"Just a ttsor. It gave us warning of the flood. If it hadn't been for that, we'd have been caught—"

"And so would we." Larsen pulled at the sodden collar of his coat. "This is a booby trap to end 'em all. What about the boys downstream?"

"Sent 'em a message," Soong answered. "Whether they got it in time—" There was no need for him to complete that sentence.

A faint hail came from across the canyon and they sighted a waving arm. Bogate carefully levered himself to his feet.

"Hooooah!" His bull roar rang out.

There was a welcome answer, three of them. But there was no way to cross the turbulent river and join forces. So they began to travel back toward the forks in two parties, the water between. Kana and Soong still had their rifles but their packs were gone. The chill air stiffened the wet clothing on the Combatants' shivering bodies. At the sinking of the sun they crouched in a hollow between two pinnacles of rock where the worst of the wind blasts were fended off, and so spent the night. Once a mournful, lowering call echoed down from the peaks. Kana took it for the hunting cry of a ttsor. But the presence of that lionlike creature here argued that, for all its apparent barrenness, there was life to be found in the badlands. For the ttsors ate not only meat but fruit and grains—perhaps here they raided the mountainside villages of the Cos.

If the Combatants slept that night it was under the drug of sheer exhaustion. And when Kana roused with the coming of light his legs and arms were so painfully cramped that he had to pinch and beat life back into his numb limbs. But across the canyon one of the other refugees waved a salute from a headland.

They began again that creeping journey along the jagged teeth of the heights. Below the river still spun, flicking around the old slides. And, even as Kana watched, a section of the cliff wall, undermined, gave way—tossing rocks and clay out into the current. So warned, they back-tracked from the rim. But here, for every mile of progress east, they traveled almost as much over or around obstacles, skirting side chasms, flanking butts and peaks. It was snail journeying and their hands left smears of blood on the stone. Even the incredibly tough Sirian reptile hide of their boots showed scars and scratches.

And a fear which none mentioned rode them. That morning when Soong had tried to reach the Horde with the speecher he had raised no answer. At every rest interval while they panted in the thin air, he bent over the obstinate machine, fingering the keys with relentless energy, but never getting a faint click in reply.

Kana thought he knew what had happened, his imagination painting a very stark picture. The Horde had come up the river bed—to meet head on that flood, speeding even more as the ground sloped. The Terran force must have been caught, to be swept away to as final an end as the older Llor army had met in the valley of bones!

So vivid was this picture that, as they approached the fork, Kana lagged behind, unwilling to look for the debris of such destruction. But Soong's shout of discovery drew him against his will.

One of the light carts was jammed into the rocks just below them, twisted almost out of shape. Bogate's wide shoulders sagged as he hunched perilously over to view the wreckage. While they stared at the evidence which blighted their hopes, a wild shout drew their attention across to where those on the other side of the river were excitedly pointing behind them at the other fork. Bogate straightened, his lusty strength coming back.

"Maybe some of 'em made it!"

Two of the scouts on the other side had disappeared, but the third continued to wave.

"The problem of getting across remains," Larsen pointed out. "We can't swim that—"

"We got across the other river, didn't we?" Soong demanded. "What we did once we can do again."

They could do anything now! The knowledge that some of the Horde must have escaped was a stimulant which sent them to perch on stones just above water level while Bogate lowered one of the rifles, stock first, to test the pull of the river, only to have it almost ripped out of his graps.

Across the water a knot of men appeared, among them Hansu. They were burdened with coils of rope and split into two groups, leaving one directly across from the marooned scouts. The Blademaster and the others went upstream, uncoiling rope as they clambered above the water line.

Here the gap, through which the water must enter the wider bed, was deeper and narrower than at any other point along its sweep from the falls. Hansu's men fastened the rope end to an unwieldy bundle and tossed it into the flood. Soong and Bogate, rifles ready, lay belly down on the rocks. The bundle flashed downstream and the rifles plunged in to capture it. There was a breathless instant when it seemed that it might escape—then all four of them had it and the rope end it brought them was safely in their hands, linking them to the party across the river.

To fight through those few feet of water was a nightmare of effort. In his turn Kana brought up against a half-sunken rock with force enough to make his head swim with pain. Then hands reached out to drag him in. Coughing up brackish water, he lay on a spit of gravel until they pulled him to his feet. The rest of the trip to the other valley was a mechanical obeying of orders, of being led. And he did not really rouse until he found himself lying on his back, a pack under his head, while Mic and Rey stripped off his soaked clothing and rubbed him down with a blanket.

Mic scowled. "What'd you do up there—blow a dam?"

"Sprung a trap—I think," Kana sputtered the words over a cup of hot brew Rey thrust upon him. There was a fire blazing not too far away and the glow of warmth within and without his shivering body was pure luxury.

"So. Well, we have one of the trappers—"

Kana's eyes followed Mic's finger. Across the fire squatted a figure neither Llor nor Terran. About four feet tall, the creature was almost completely covered with a thick growth of gray-white hair. About its loins was a brief kilt of supple ttsor fur and it wore a thong necklet from which depended several thumb claws of the same felines. Even more expressionless than the less woolly Llor, the prisoner stared unblinkingly into the fire and paid little or no attention to his surroundings.

"Cos?"

"We think so. We caught him feeding a signal fire up on the cliffs night before last. But so far we haven't been able to get anything out of him. He doesn't answer to trade talk, and even Hansu's Llor can't bring an answer out of him. We pull him along, he sits when we stop—he won't eat—"

As he talked Mic opened his pack and pulled out spare clothing while Rey contributed more. Kana gratefully donned the donations, watching his own clothes steam before the fire.

"Good thing our warning reached you in time—"

Mic did not quite meet his eyes. "The flood caught five of the men—a cart got hung up on a rock and they were working to free it. Then we lost three crossing the first river and a couple when the fur faces jumped us later—"

"The Llor followed you?"

"Part way. They faded out when we reached the bone valley. I suppose that gave them an idea of what they could expect. Anyway they chased us in and there's no going back that way—unless we want to fight the whole nation. The rebels are all loyal royalists now and only too ready to attack the nasty Terran invaders—" There was a bitter undertone to that.

"What's it like up ahead?" Rey wanted to know.

Swiftly Kana outlined what he had seen. As he spoke their faces grew bleak. But before he had finished Hansu strode up to the fire.

"See any Cos signs above the falls before that water came?" the Bladmaster demanded.

"No, sir. We saw nothing but a ttsor and it gave us the

alarm. I'd laid out a trade packet on a rock because we felt as if we were being watched. The ttsor came down to look it over and then——"

But Hansu was staring across the flames at the captive Cos. "All we need to know is locked up in that round skull over there—if we could just pry it out. But he won't eat our food, he won't talk. And we can't keep him until he starves. Then they would have good reason to strike back at us."

The Blademaster went around to stand beside the prisoner. But the white-wooled pygmy never changed position nor gave any indication that he was aware of the Terran commander. Hansu went down on one knee, slowly repeating some words in the sing-song speech of the Llor. The Cos did not even blink. Kana reached for the trade packets he had carried so long, made a hasty selection, and passed on a small package of sugar and a stone-set wrist band.

Hansu held the gemmed circlet into the light before the sullen captive, turning it so that the stones flashed. The offering might have been totally invisible as far as the Cos was concerned. Nor when the sugar cake was held within sniffing distance did he make any move to investigate. To him the Terrans and their gifts did not exist.

"He's a stone wall and we're up against him," Hansu said. "We can only——"

"Let him go, sir, and hope for the best?" Kana's X-Tee training suggested that.

"Yes." Hansu stood up and then pulled the Cos to his feet. Compelling the captive by his great strength, the Blademaster marched the pygmy to the edge of the Terran camp and a good hundred yards beyond. Then he released the mountaineer's arm and stepped away.

For a long space the Cos remained exactly where he had been left—he did not even turn his head to see if they were watching him. Then, with a skittering movement, the speed of which left the Combatants agape, he was gone,

vanishing at the far side of the canyon. Somewhere a stone
rattled, but they saw nothing of the trail he took.

The Horde camped there for that night and, though
they watched the mountains ahead and the cliffs walling
them in, there were no more signal fires.

"Maybe," Mic suggested hopefully, "uncorking that
river was their biggest gun. When they saw that it didn't
work, they went into hiding, to let us gallop by—"

"We don't know how their minds work," Kana warned.
"To some species—take ours for example—a failure such
as that is merely a spur to try again. To another type it
would signify that their Gods, or Fate, or whatever Power
they believe in, is opposed and they should forget the
whole project. The future may depend upon that Cos we
freed and the report he makes. But we shall have to be
prepared for anything."

Soon after the march began the next morning they
passed the site where the byll had been killed. The carcass
had been torn apart and largely devoured by unseen scav-
angers in the night. But the severed head, with its toothed
bill gaping, was a grim warning. One of the duties of the
flankers was to keep close watch against sneak attacks
from the carnivorous birds.

Close to mid-day they came upon a pool fed by water
seeping through the left canyon wall, perhaps from the
river flowing down the other fork. Here they filled their
canteens after purifying the liquid and washed some of the
dust from their hands and faces. This grit, borne by the
wind, was in their mouths as they ate, inflamed their eyes,
and sifted down between clothing and skin to prove a
minor torture.

Alert to the danger which might come from above, the
scouts reported a second major attack before it got under-
way. The Cos, relying upon methods which had served
them well in the past, sent boulders crashing down. But
none of the rough missiles killed, for those who attempted
to so bombard the winding snake of the Horde's advance

were picked off by sharpshooting flankers and woolly bodies crashed along with the rocks while others fled. Ahead, on a mesa-like formation, was a rude fortification which so commanded their line of march that the Terrans dared not try to pass.

This time the Cos made no attempt to hide their presence. With the coming of evening beacons blazed in the fort—forming a barrier of light about it much as the camp lamps of the Combatants had done for them on the plains. There could be no storming this from below. Facing the Horde the rise to the mesa top was steep and an ominous row of boulders ready for use fringed the rim. Hansu whistled for a gathering.

"We have to take that fort," he began baldly. "And there's only one way in—from the top." He took off his helmet and threw into it black and white pebbles. "Lot-choice—"

Lot-choice it was. Kana grabbed a pebble with the rest, holding it concealed in his hand until the word of command. In that moment he found that the stone he held was black, as was Rey's—while Mic, to his disappointment, had a white one.

Hansu gave a detailed inspection to the band who were to make the climb. The volunteers stripped themselves of all trappings except one belt. Their rifles were slung over their shoulders and each man wore his sword-knife and carried five of the explosive fire cartridges.

They used the deep shadows at the floor of the canyon to cloak their withdrawal from the main command, back-tracking on their path of the afternoon to a point where the flankers had reported the cliffs scalable. There, utilizing the last scrap of twilight before the night clamped down, they started up. And, once on top, the fort lights not only provided them with a guide but a certain amount of illumination. Their advance was a slow creep. To run into a Cos sentry would be fatal, and as a warning of that the Terrans had their sense of smell—luckily the wind blew toward them. The oily body odor of the Llor, distinguishable at several feet by off-world noses, was multiplied fourfold in that given off by the Cos. The mountaineers could literally be smelled out of ambush, a betrayal of which they were not aware.

The ominous reek filled Kana's nostrils. He drew his legs under him and reached out to tap Rey's shoulder, knowing that that silent warning would be passed down the crawling Terran line. A Cos was ahead, slightly to the left. With his head raised to follow the scent, Kana wriggled on. He felt Rey's fingers on his ankle as the other joined him. The Cos must be located and eliminated, efficiently and without giving any warning to the fort.

Kana lined up a neighboring pinnacle with the lights of the fort. His nose told him that the Cos must be there, and it was a logical position from which to watch not only the cliff but the Horde below.

Then he saw what he was searching for—a blob of black outlined against the fort beacons, the hunched head and shoulders of the mountaineer sentry. Kana tensed for a spring as he unhooked the carrying strap of his rifle. With that timing and precision in attack he had been drilled in for most of his life, he uncoiled in a leap, bringing the strap about the woolly throat of the sentry. A single jerk in the proper direction and the Cos went limp. Kana eased the body to the ground with shaking hands. The trick had worked—just as the instructors had assured them that it would. But between trying it on a dummy and on a living, breathing creature there was a vast gulf of sensation. He pulled the strap away with a twitch and rubbed his hands along his thighs, trying to free his flesh from the feel of greasy wool.

"All right?"

"Yes," he answered Rey and took the rifle the other offered him, making a business of re-attaching the strap.

There were no more sentries sighted. And at last the

Terran force gained the point they wished—to the west and above the fort.

The center building of that eagles' nest was familiar in shape, though in bad repair. When the Cos had taken over this stronghold they used for its core an earlier fortification or outpost erected by the Llor. The handful of brush and stone huts grouped around the half-ruined watchtower and the wall of loose stones were their own additions—neither displaying any great skill in military engineering.

From below sounded the shrilling of Terran battle whistles. And by the fires of the Cos they could see the white forms of the mountaineers manning the wall, levering into place their rocky ammunition, ready to roll it down to meet any frontal attack. Kana snapped open one of the fire cartridges and pitched it at the nearest brush-roofed hut.

To the yellow flames of the Cos beacons was added the bursting stars of the Terran fire balls, flaring up to turn the fort into an inferno. The startled Cos, caught between the Horde below and this new menace, ran back and forth. And that moment of indecision finished them, though the end did not come from the Terran attackers but from within their own stronghold.

Out of the fires a black shadow came to life, sweeping straight up into the night. It hovered over the fort and red death rained from it. Cos, their wool afire, plunged blind and screaming over the drop or ran to meet death head on. But the strange flying thing spiraled skyward, flitting over the valley to lay more bombs in the ranks of the Horde.

The Terrans on the heights tried to catch the swooping wing in the sights of their rifles, firing in wild fury at its outline. Under their concentrated blast the wing staggered, tried to level off, and then hurtled on into the night, leaving a scarlet path of destruction which not only engulfed the fortress of the Cos but the Horde pocketed below.

9

SHOW OUR TEETH AND HOPE

At dawn the Terran force held the fort, but the price had been high. A quarter of the Horde had either died quickly in the bombing raid of the unknown plane or were granted grace for hideous wounds during the hours which followed. So the victory bore more the shade of a defeat.

"Where did the Cos get that wing?" Mic, his left arm a roll of shielding plasta-flesh to his shoulder, was not the only one to ask that.

The alien machine was proof that there must have been strangers hidden in the Cos stronghold, either inciting the mountaineers against the Terrans, or as spectators. Combatants inspected the ruins of the fort while parts of it still blazed, searching for evidence of the origin of the flyers, but the flames had left them no readable clues.

"That wing never got away unharmed," Rey reiterated to any who would listen. "It must have crashed—it was sideslipping when it went out of sight!"

"Where there's one of those," Mic returned, "there're probably more. Space demons! With those they can fly over and dust us whenever they want to! But why haven't they done that before?"

Kana put a pack behind Mic's good shoulder and settled

him back against that support. "Lack of supplies may be
the answer. Probably they haven't enough machines to
chase us. We forced that one into the open by firing the
fort huts. And I think Rey's right, it crashed on ahead.
Anyway—from here on we don't have to march down the
middle of a canyon, providing them with a perfect target."

For that was the Terrans' greatest discovery—the well-
defined road running along the cliff straight west from the
Cos fort. And Hansu was determined to get his mangled
command up out of what might prove to be a deathtrap.
The Combatants licked their wounds and explored the
fort, sending scouts out along the road, well into the second day. The number of Cos bodies found within the en-
closure were fewer than they expected and there were no
Aliens among them.

"An expendable rearguard," Hansu deduced.

In the end the corpses of the enemy were carried to the
small central area of the fort and given the same burial
granted the Terran dead—total destruction in the flames.
Beneath ground level, in a chamber hollowed from the
rock of the mountain, they found a cistern of water and a
line of bins filled with grain and dried fruits. The grain
could not be eaten by Terrans, Medico Crawfur announced, but the fruit was not harmful and they chewed
its leathery substance as a welcome variation to ration tablets.

On the third day they reorganized and combined the
shrunken teams and took up the march in good order. But
there was no longer any talk about a quick return to Secundus. By unspoken consent discussion of the future was
limited to that day's journey and vague speculation concerning the next.

"Just show our teeth and hope—" was the way Mic put
it as he started out between Kana and Rey. "If we could
only get out of this blasted tangle of rocks!"

But there was no end to the rocks as the trail from the
fort climbed higher. Taking his turn Kana became one of

the scouts ranging ahead. They were working their way up
the slope of a peak which had once been volcanic. And
now patches of snow laced the ground. Kana chanced
upon a break in the wall of that cone, a place where they
might normally expect opposition. But the pass was unde-
fended. And accompanied by Soong he halted to look
down into a hollow, the deepest part of which lay at least a
Terran mile below. Cupped there was a lake and the yellow-green of Fronnian flora patterned small, regular fields,
while a village of stone-walled, domed huts clustered by
the water. Nothing moved in those fields, no smoke hung
above the village. It might have been deserted an hour—
or a century—before.

The scouts spread out, making their way down the side
of the bowl—alert and ready. But all they flushed out of
the tall grass was a khat, one of the striped rodents that
furnished the main meat supply of Fronn. Crossing small
fields carpeted with the stiff stubble of grain, they came to
the lake.

Soong pointed to the shore line where deep marks were
scored in the mud.

"Boats— And not too long ago."

"Can't see any. Maybe they went that way—"

A long finger of water angled south toward the wall of
the crater. Whether it washed the outer wall of the cone
they could not be sure. But no boats were to be seen. And
further exploration proved that, save for a khat or two,
and four small guen penned in a corral, the valley was
empty.

So the Horde came down in peace. The finger of lake
draining south was discovered to enter a break in the wall
and from signs the Terrans were inclined to believe that
the inhabitants of the valley had fled in that direction.

But the most exciting discovery was made just beyond
the village—a mass of wreckage—the flying wing! No evidence of the other-world origin of the pilot remained. But

the machine was not Terran Mech—as they had suspected all along.

Their nearest to an expert on machines, El Kosti, spent several hours pulling at the jumble of wires and metal with a company of Combatants to lend assistance.

"This came from Sirius II," he reported to Hansu. "But there are modifications I can't identify. I'd say it might originally have been a trade scout—though I couldn't swear to it. But it is not Terran stuff."

Back again to the thought that there was some cloudy conspiracy—that C.C. was moving against them. Why? Because they were Terran mercenaries? Kana wondered about that. Was Yorke's Horde with its quantity of trained veterans marked down in someone's book as being expendable—to be wiped out so that its loss would cause trouble back home? Was pressure thus being brought to bear to force mankind out of space? He watched Hansu taking careful visa shots of the wreck as Kosti pointed out those portions of the machine which most clearly indicated its probable origin. The Blademaster was collecting evidence—but would he ever be allowed to present it to the authorities? Did he honestly believe that any of them would reach Secundus—let alone stand in Prime's hall of justice to testify to this act of treachery?

Hut by hut they searched the village. Only trash remained in the rooms, along with pieces of furniture too large or heavy for refugees to move. Three explorer ration paks were discovered in the refuse. Proving that at least one other-world visitor had been there recently. But these were standard paks which revealed nothing about the one who had used them—he could have been from one of twenty different planets.

Without boats or the means of making a raft the Terrans could not use the water exit from the crater valley. But there was a second road leading on south-west and they took it. From that day on the march became a nightmare. The windy season was on them and the storms brought swirling clouds of snow to hide the trail. Some of the men were lost in a single hour's march, dropping out of line never to be sighted again, in spite of the efforts to keep the lines moving and intact. Some frankly gave up, could not be beaten to their feet after a rest, drifting into that fatal sleep which meant death. Had they not been mercenary trained, bred to severe physical strain from their childhood, perhaps none of them would have won through. As it was they lost fifty men before they came to the western slopes of the range. Now the mere fact that they were going down again, with the plains of Tharc before them, gave them a renewal of spirit and kept them going on stumbling feet.

At least they had had to fight only one thing at a time. Since the battle at the fort they had not sighted the Cos. The mountaineers must have gone into hiding during the storms.

On the fifth day after they left the crater valley, Kana, weaving weakly as he set one foot carefully before the other, made his way down a ravine and crossed bare ground, glad to miss the crunch of snow. The walls of the tiny valley cut off the worst of the wind and he leaned against the bank to catch his breath. A trickle of water flowed past him southwest.

"Down!" He said the word aloud, savoring it, enjoying its meaning. Now the mountains lay behind, the plains were open to them.

But not yet were they out of the broken "badlands" which encumbered this side of the range also. In the wilderness of mesas and knife-edged valleys there were the colored splotches of vegetation, growing quickly on the moisture fed by the winds. But there was no discernible sign of a road or of any other evidence of civilization. They could only continue to march south, heading for the level land enclosing Tharc.

Kana stumbled along beside the thread of stream, following the defile simply because he could not now summon the strength necessary to climb out of the ravine. Plants uncurled leaves to the sun. A spray of tiny green blossoms, hung on delicate, lacy stems, bowed to meet the water.

"Yaah—!"

Kana came around in a half crouch, his rifle ready, to see Soong pick himself out of the stream, swearing at the greasy mud. Looking up at Kana his round ivory face split in a grin which was wide and ready.

"We have come out of winter into spring. Now I think we shall live."

"For a while," Kana conceded thoughtfully. He was tired, so tired he wanted to drop down on the earth where he stood and rest—forever.

"Yes, we live. And perhaps that shall disappoint some. Ho, now a river—in truth a river!"

Soong was right. The tricklet spilled out to join a river. Here the flood ran clear so that the Terrans could see the flat stones and gravel which floored its bottom. And the watery reach lacked the fury of the mountain courses they had met.

"Not deep—this one we can wade. Fortune displays a smiling face at last!" Soong squatted down and ventured to test the temperature of the fluid with a forefinger, withdrawing it quickly. "Born in snow, yes. We shall have very cold feet—"

They walked along the bank for a distance. Out of the withered drifts of last season's grass a khat exploded with a muffled snuffle of panic. It skidded to the edge of the water, slipped on clay and, wildly kicking, plunged over. Its struggles continued in the water, keeping it afloat.

From the opposite bank shot a vee of ripples heading for that point of disturbance. The khat shrieked, a cry of agony almost human with pain and terror. Blood rilled out to stain the water and other lines of ripples converged toward it.

The Combatants stood aghast at the sight. But the struggle ceased seconds after it had begun. On the stones at the bottom lay clean picked bones.

Lazily, glutted, three small forms floated. They were six-limbed, frog-headed creatures, but their jaws were the jaws of rapacious carnivora, and their four eyes, set in a double row above those vicious jaws, were black beads of ferocious, intelligent hunger.

Kana moistened his lips. "Tif."

"What—?" Soong shied a stone at the small monsters. They glided off a foot or two, but they did not return to the opposite bank. Instead they lingered just out of range, their attention fixed on the Terrans—waiting—watching—

"Bad news," Kana answered Soong's half question. "You saw what happened to that khat. Well, that will happen to any living thing that tries to cross water where tif live."

"But there're only three and none of them are more than a foot long—"

"Three of them we can see. And where there're three —there're more. They travel in schools. Three in sight may well mean three hundred in cover, ready to attack when there's meat enough!"

No, there was no way of judging how many of the frog-devils infested the river. And there was no practical way of getting across a stream so guarded. If the record-pak on Prime had not been so limited in its information! Or if the Terrans only had friendly natives to provide them with advice.

The limpid water seemed very peaceful, but as the Combatants moved downstream the tif swam effortlessly to parallel their path. Now and then the little monsters were joined by others of their species, come from the shadows below the banks, who paddled out to confer with the three in mid-stream, eye the Terrans for themselves, as if estimating their bulk, before retreating again to their hidden dens.

"Spreading the word—meat on the hoof—" Kana stopped.

The shallow river had widened as they followed it south, and now it was islanded with dry-topped rocks forming an irregular path. The Terran scout studied these —stepping stones? Could some sort of net be rigged above and below to keep off the tif? A few of the men might be able to cross here, leaping from rock to rock. But the whole Horde, burdened with disabled and wounded, could not do it. The problem would have to be turned over to that handful of experts in survival Hansu had gathered on his staff—veterans who pooled knowledge gained on a hundred different worlds to keep them and their comrades alive on this one.

But suddenly the breeze brought a familiar reek to his nostrils. He had not scented that since the night at the Cos fort. Kana threw himself down behind a bush and Soong landed beside him a moment later.

Almost directly across the river a tall Llor rode out on a sand spit. He carried no lance but balanced an air rifle across his saddle, thus proclaiming his rank as a regular of the royalist guard, rather than a warrior-follower of some provincial noble. The trooper dismounted to approach the water gingerly, inspecting the ripples before he struck down into them with the butt of his weapon. Plainly he was aware of the tif.

But safe on the sand he sat cross-legged, taking out a length of purple cane to chew while he waited. The Terrans flattened themselves every time the Llor's glance swung carelessly across their too-thin cover. There was no hope of withdrawing unseen now.

The Llor spat pieces of pulped cane into the water and once or twice threw stones at the clustering tif. More and more ripples headed for that tongue of gravel as beneath the surface the small masters of the river gathered. Now and then the Llor watched them and gave birth to that snorting sound which served his race for laughter. But,

Kana noted, he was careful to stay away from the water.

A mewling cry brought the trooper to his feet. Out of the woods came a party of riders. The one in the van wore a short scarlet cloak lined with ttsor fur and carried before him on a perch attached to his saddle a trained hork—thus identifying himself as a member of the Gatanu's own household. But among the other riders was the hooded, robed figure of a Ventur.

The noble did not dismount, but his guard did, pulling the trader with them. For, astonishingly enough, the Ventur was a prisoner, his hands lashed at his back. The Llor held a conference with their scout, their leader going so far as to ride out on the spit to peer curiously into the water, while the guards urged their captive to the bank.

Then, to the horror of the watching Terrans, they calmly picked up the smaller trader and flung him into the stream where the water was now whipped to a foam by the swarming tif.

Kana's first avenging shot snapped the noble out of his saddle—to plunge into the river headfirst. Methodically the Terrans fired in volleys, picking off the murderers on the far bank. Five of the party were down before the other three fled for the protection of the trees. But none of the fugitives reached that grove.

There was a continued flurry in the water where the tif greeted this rare abundance of meat. Kana dared not look at the place where the helpless Ventur had fallen. Death in battle was commonplace—he had been trained to believe that it would be his own end. But the callous cruelty he had just witnessed was to him a terrifying thing.

"By Klem and Kol'." Soong twitched at his sleeve and pointed to the river.

Something struggled there, flopping about—hampered by sodden robe and bound hands. And in an ever-widening circle about the Ventur floated tif, limp and belly up. Kana leaped to the top of the nearest rock and then to the next. A stripped Llor skull snarled up at him as he jumped the water gap which cradled it. The Ventur was on his feet, winding toward the sand spit where a moment later Kana and Soong joined him. Kana drew his knife.

"I cut those—" he said in the trade tongue, motioning to the hide thongs which bound the other's arms.

The Ventur retreated a step. His struggle to gain the shore had not dislodged his masking hood. Unable to read anything from the gray expanse, broken only by the eye-holes, Kana did not follow him.

"Friend—" Kana used that word with all the emphasis he could give it. He pointed to what was left of the Llor noble. "Enemy of us—enemy of you—"

The Ventur might be considering that point. Suddenly he wheeled and backed toward the Terrans, extending his bound wrists as far as he could. Kana sawed through the wet thongs.

His hands free, the Ventur caught the dangling reins of the noble's mount. An unusually well-trained and therefore highly valued animal, it had not bolted with the rest. The Ventur mounted somewhat awkwardly. His hooded head turned from the river to the bodies of the Llor on its banks and the skeletons in the water where the tif, replete, still floated, their menacing eyes on the prey they could not reach.

One hand groped beneath the robe and came out with a small damp bag. A finger which was closer to a green-gray claw indicated the lazily swimming death and then the inert bodies of the tif which had threatened *it*. It motioned as if sowing something from the bag on the stream. When Kana nodded, the bag was tossed to him and the Ventur kicked the gu into a racking gallop back into the woods.

"Is that something to knock out the tif?" Soong questioned. "Do you suppose they knew he had it when they threw him in?"

"I don't think so, or they would have taken it from him.

Maybe its effects are permanent—those floating over there haven't come to—"

The tif which had attacked the Ventur to their own undoing still drifted belly-up, their wicked mouths open. And Kana noticed that their active fellows avoided them. The bag in his hand might grant the Horde a safe crossing.

And so it did. The gritty white powder it contained, strewn on the water upstream, kept off the tif until the Terran force was across. Whether the poison had a permanent effect the Combatants never learned, but as the rearguard trailed through the shallows tif bodies bumped the stepping stones and washed ashore on the spit.

Hansu identified the insignia of the Llor dead as that of the Household Corps. But he was more interested in the trouble between the Ventur and the guardsmen. The great deference paid the hooded ones on the march of Skura's troops east had underlined the belief that then the Llor wanted in no way to antagonize their silent transport specialists. Yet now a Llor noble had calmly ordered one of the Venturi thrown to a horrible death. Somehow the balance of power must have shifted amazingly during the days when the Horde had been fighting across the mountains—shifted to embolden the Llor to show an arrogant contempt for those they had respected for generations. Events certainly suggested that the Llor now had backing so strong that they believed they could make themselves the undisputed rulers of all Fronn. And was that support more than a renegade Mech Legion?

As the Combatants marched on, through valleys which spread out to the level lands of the plains, their alert uneasiness increased. Here the armored, moving fortresses of the Mechs could operate to the greatest advantage. Scouts spent hours each day watching the sky as well as the country before them for signs of aircraft. But since the clash with the party of Llor at the tif river they sighted no enemy. This land appeared to be left to the ttsor, the byll, and the wild khat upon which the two preyed.

On the second day after the Terrans had crossed the river their scouts sighted a village. It was a small frontier, semi-fortress, ringed with corrals where the wild guen of these northern plains were rounded up once a year, sorted, and the duo-yearlings sold after a minimum of training. The pens were full now and a mounted force could move faster. Hansu decided it was wise to turn cavalry and the Combatants altered their line of march, heading for the town.

10

TO THE SEA

As the Horde spread out in a half-arc across the eastern approach to the town, the first signs of life, other than the restless guen in the corrals, showed in a band of Llor, some riding, some trudging humbly on foot, headed from the domed houses toward the Terran lines. The foremost rider waved over his head a hastily constructed parley flag.

Remembering the fate of Yorke and his officers, neither Hansu nor any other of the Combatants moved from the cover they had taken on the first sight of the Llor. Apparently disconcerted by meeting with only empty landscape the Llor leader reined in his gu and sat, waving the flag at the brush and trees, his followers clustered timidly about him—trying to face in all directions at once.

"Lords—War Lords of Terra—" called the leader, addressing the empty air. And his words lengthened oddly until "Terra" might well have been "terror."

Without rising to view Hansu answered:

"What would you, Corban?" giving the other the honorary title of a headman of a city.

"What would *you*, Lords of Terra?" countered the Llor. He handed the flag to one of his companions and sat, his hands on his thighs, facing in the direction of the Blademaster's voice. "Do you bring us war?"

"We war only when it is offered us. Where open hands hold no swords, we show palms in return. We but wish to travel the road to our homes."

The Llor swung out of his saddle and started to the Terran lines. One of his followers attempted to detain him, only to be pushed aside as the Fronnian, his hands held ostentatiously before him, advanced.

"My hands are open, Lord. I close no road to you."

Hansu arose to meet him, holding his own palms up.

"What would you then, Corban?"

"Word that my village will not be trodden into the earth, nor the blood of my people shaken wet from your swords, War Lord."

"Has not the war banner been raised against us?" countered the Blademaster.

"Lord, what have little men to do with the fine words of Gatanus and nobles? He who sits on the hork-winged bench means little to us—there are always those to gather taxes in his name, whatever it may be. We wish only to live and depart not into the Dark Mists before our time. And stern things have been said of you off-world ones— that you fight with fire those who deny you what you would take. Therefore come I to treat with you for the life of my village. Grain is yours, and the fruits of our fields— and whatever else you wish. Guen also—if it be your will to strip our pens of the newly caught wild ones. Only take your fill and go!"

"Then what if the Gatanu's men come and say unto you, 'You have fed the enemy and given him guen to ride upon. You are one with him'?"

The Corban shook his head. "How can they in truth say that? For you are an army of men trained in strange and horrible forms of warfare. Nay, all of Fronn knows that nothing can stand against the might of your sword arms. For you fight not only blade to blade after our custom, but with fire which sears from a great distance and with death rained from the air. Some of you crawl in mighty for-

tresses of metal, lying snug within their bellies as they
creep across the ground and crush your enemies under
their weight! These things are widely known. So the Gatanu's men cannot believe that a village guard would dare
deny you anything you desired. Therefore, I entreat you,
Lord, take what you will and go—leaving us our lives!"

"You have seen the Terran fortresses which creep, the
machines which fly through the air?"

"Not with my eyes, Lord. For I am an outland man—
though Corban of men who do not flinch from hunting the
ttsor on foot, nor from snaring the guen of the dales. But
in the south all men have seen these wonders and the word
has spread to our ears."

"These are then to be found about Tharc?"

"Yes, Lord, there are many of your wonderful machines there now. You wish to join them? It is well. But I
entreat you—take what you want and go."

Hansu dropped his empty hands. "Good enough. We
shall not invade your village, Corban. Send us supplies and
one hundred guen—those broken to saddle use. And we
shall not be deceived if you give us wild ones, but if you
do we shall come and choose for ourselves."

The Corban raised his hands to his breast and then to
his forehead in the salute a vassal renders his lord. "War
Lord, it shall be even as you say. We shall bring you a
conqueror's share and thank you for your mercy."

The Llor party went back to the village and Hansu addressed the shrunken Horde.

"—that's the picture. From this fellow's description
there must be a full Mech Legion at Tharc. They have
heavy stuff as well as wings with them."

"What about Truce Law?" called a voice from the
ranks.

"Let's face it. Truce Law was broken when they flamed
Yorke and the rest. Mech renegades aren't alone in this
—they couldn't have brought in heavy stuff without help
—a lot of it. And now they believe that they can settle us

whenever they wish. I don't care how much backing they have—they don't dare let any news of this get back to Prime. So their first move will be so shut us away from the ships at Tharc."

Shut off from Tharc—bottled up on Fronn—unable to get away. Kana watched the uncertainty mirrored on the faces of those about him begin to change to something else —a grim determination. Generations ago the weaklings, the irresolute, had been weeded and bred out of the Combatant strain. The mercenaries were, by the very nature of their trade, fatalists. Few lived to retire, or even to go into semi-service at the base. And they had followed many lost causes to the end. But this was a new experience. The code which to them was a creed, an unshakable belief, had been flouted. And for that someone was going to pay!

"We'll get 'em—" The words were drowned out in a growl of assent.

But Hansu's gesture silenced that. "We're not alone," he reminded them. "Once Combat Law is broken here, what will happen? Others will begin to set Mech against Arch."

He did not need to continue. They knew what that would mean—vicious civil war on half a thousand planets, one Terran force pitted against another, bleeding their own world white—

"That has to be stopped here and now. One message to Combat Center and it will be!"

"We can't face up to big stuff in the field!" someone shouted.

"We won't try to. But we've got to get a messenger to Secundus or Prime. And the rest of us must hole up and wait for Combat to move."

"Stay in the mountains?" There was no enthusiasm in that question. They had had enough of Fronn's mountains.

Hansu shook his head. "We have an alternative. First we must learn more about what is going on. Now—set hostile country camp. Swordtans, scouts, report to me."

They went to the duties in which they had been drilled. Kana joined the others at the cart where Hansu waited for them. The commander had spread out a much-creased sheet of skin and was frowning at the blue lines which crossed and re-crossed its surface.

"Bogate"—he turned to the head scout—"when that Corban comes out with supplies, round him up and bring him here. These guen hunters must know the land for miles, know it intimately. We want all the information about it we can pry out of them. Mechs can't operate in rough territory—so we've got to keep to broken wilderness."

"But all around Tharc is open plain," one of the Swordtans objected.

"We have no intention of going to Tharc. They'll be watching for us to try that."

"The only space port—"

Hansu corrected him instantly. "The only *military* space port is at Tharc. You are forgetting the Venturi!"

Kana's lips shaped a soundless whistle. The Blademaster was right. The Venturi! As hereditary traders of Fronn they had some centers of their own on the mainland. And not too far from the western sea was a small off-world space landing used by the few alien traders who had managed to establish contact with the Venturi for a limited exchange of goods—mostly exotic novelties the Fronnian merchants were suspected of reselling at fabulous profit. To reach there—to take control of one of the trading ships —that offered a better chance than to try to blast their way into the toothed trap which was now Tharc.

"There is a space port near the Venturi holdings at Po'ult," Hansu was explaining. "There is no regular schedule of ships, but off-world traders do come. And we may have luck in making a deal for shelter with the Venturi. If we head straight west we should strike the sea not far from Po'ult."

The Corban was only too willing to provide any assis-

:ance which would insure getting these dangerous Terrans
ɔut of his territory. Kneeling with two of his best guen
ιunters over the map Hansu had produced, he asked one
ϙuestion which the Blademaster had to parry adroitly.

"But why, Lord, must you seek out a path through this
wilderness? To the south the road is wide and smooth and
:here your brothers await you."

"It is our wish to visit the Venturi of the coast—and not
:o come upon them by a well-marked road—"

The Llor's tiny circle of a mouth moved in the Fronnian
equivalent of a smile.

"Ha. Then it is true—that which has been whispered
from mouth to ear—that the day of reckoning with *those*
is coming? No longer shall the hooded ones keep the trails,
nor be the only buyers and sellers to carry goods from one
village to the next! That is good to hear, Lord. Eat up the
Venturi forts along the coast if you will—and all the Llor
shall speak kindly of you to the Ruler of the Winds. For
when those fall, then there shall be rich spoil for all."

Eagerly he consulted the map. "Now here is a path—it
lies among the western mountains and there may be Cos.
But to *you* what are Cos—you may brush them out of
your way as we brush the fas-fas beetles from our floors.
And this path will lead you directly to the sea above
Po'ult. May your hunting there prosper, War Lord!"

"Indeed may it," piously returned Hansu. And he
moved his fingers in the Three Signs of those air, fire, and
water spirits who must be consulted on Fronn before any
major undertaking.

The Corban warmed still more and became their cham-
pion with the guen herders, personally inspecting the stock
his fellow citizens had run out from the village corrals, and
rejecting ten animals, much to the bafflement of his men
who were prepared to make a handsome profit from the
ignorance of off-world men, for Hansu insisted on paying
for the animals. That night he gave a feast, using a
month's supplies with the abandon of a Chortha of a prov-

ince. To the future conquerors of the Venturi he would deny nothing. And a handpicked corps of guides, selected from the most hardy and far roving of the guen hunters, was detailed to accompany the Horde to the foothills of the western mountains.

That was a day and a half journey—mounted—and Hansu pushed them to the utmost, driven himself by the desire to get out of the dangerous level country before they were sighted by a Mech patrol.

On the morning of the third day when they were well on the mountain trail they found the Llor guides gone. Distant behind them was the smudge of smoke in the sky and bits of charred grass drifted down. The hunters had lighted a plains fire to drive the wild guen into a netting place. Hansu watched that haze with satisfaction. It would effectively cover their trail, which was perhaps why the Llor hunters had lit it.

Now began the old nightmare of climbing, climbing and being ever alert for an attack. Though the hunters had insisted that this route lay on the edge of Cos-held country and that the mountaineers had very seldom troubled the caravans which used it, they could not be sure of a peaceful penetration. And the Llor had been unable to answer Hansu's questions as to whether the Venturi caravanmen had some pact with the Cos which insured that safety. However, the Terrans had no alternative but to advance.

The trail was marked with those narrow stone pillars erected by the Venturi, the pictographs on them untranslatable. And it was made for the use of guen.

That night they went without fire, camped in small groups, strung out with sentries between. But the hours of darkness were not broken by alarms and they sighted no beacons on the heights.

Kana had tramped behind Hansu for most of that day, and now, his blanket pulled about him for warmth, he crouched by an outcrop trying to snatch some sleep while the Blademaster sat cross-legged a yard away and listened to the reports of scouts.

"—no deal with these Mechs?"

"Not a chance." Hansu's voice brought him fully awake. "Mills said that Hart Device was in command."

"Device! I still think Deke musta been wrong. Device wouldn't go outlaw—"

"That's just the point, Bogate. If Device is the commander at Tharc—and I see no reason not to trust information Mills died to bring us—then this is no matter of a Mech Legion gone outlaw. Hart Device is a new leader—just as Yorke was. His Legion is small but tough, well equipped, and Hart has the reputation of delivering. I'd be willing to lay half a year's pay that he has a large percentage of vets—just as we have. I wonder—" His voice trailed off.

But Kana, tired as he was, caught that hint. A Legion, a Horde, both consisting of well-trained men, locked in a death struggle. No matter which won in the end, the death toll would be high. So many veterans removed from action. It was beginning to add up to an ugly sum.

"If the Code's broke"—Zapan Bogate's rumbling whisper had thoughtful undertones—"hell's to pay! Why—Archs won't have a chance!"

"Not at the old game, no. But that is no reason why we can't start a new one."

"But—we're Combat men, Hansu—"

"Sure. Only there's no rule about who or what we have to fight." There was an absent note in the Blademaster's voice as if he were thinking aloud.

"Anyways, now we got just one job." Bogate heaved himself up. "To get outta these blasted hills and see the Venturi. We gonna try to take 'em, sir?"

"Not if we can help it. They may welcome us with open arms if what that Corban hinted is true and the Llor have turned against them. Their territory is too rough for the

Mechs. This Po'ult of theirs is built on an island off the coast—sheer rock straight up from the sea. They have their own ways of getting ashore and you can't bring up heavy stuff to batter it."

"Good place for us to hole up—if they'll let us."

"That's what we'll have to arrange, Bogate. If we can make them see we have a common enemy, maybe they'll make it a common war. Take scouts out in the morning as usual."

"Yes, sir."

At dawn the trek began again. Snow lay in patches along the trail, and the patches became solid sheets, drifting across the track, drifts through which men on foot beat a way for the slender-legged guen. But in that struggle they lost animals, for the wild, newly captured mounts were not tough enough for a battle such as this. The second cart became a casualty—and with it one of the medical corpsmen who did not have a chance to relinquish his drag rope as it slithered over the edge of a drop and plunged to a slope far below.

"Alert!" The war whistle shrieked the message along, to set numb hands unslinging rifles, freeing sword-knives. That was the only warning they had before the battle of the pass began. But now they were not tangling with Cos but with a party of Llor in flight, desperate to win through, back to the plains and safety. And because of their desperation they came on without caution, trying to hack their way through the Horde.

The struggle was a short one, the rear guard of the Horde never firing a shot. But it was bloody. For the Llor died to a man and they had been so reckless in their attack that they had cut down in their insane scramble men who would not normally have been drawn into a hand-to-hand combat.

The Terrans, already spent with their struggle through the snow to these heights, licked their wounds that night and camped, sick with weariness, on the edge of the battlefield. Wind-driven snow covered the fallen and the Combatants who could keep their feet moved among the wounded striving to ward off frozen death.

"Raiding party being chased home—" The sear breeze pulled the words from between Mic's chapped lips. "Maybe we're marching straight into a fire someone else started. Hope the Venturi won't think we're more of the same—"

Rey rubbed one cheek with a handful of snow. "Never a dull moment." He wheezed and then coughed until his whole rangy body shook. "Next time we have a premonition about any enlistment—me, I'm going to believe it! What a paradise replacement barracks was—why did I ever leave Secundus?"

Kana beat gloved hands together. Secundus seemed very far and long ago. Had he *ever* eaten in a room where flame birds flitted on the walls? Or was that a dream and this present nightmare stark reality?

"We'll just plow on and on through this"—Mic kicked a pile of snow—"until it is deep enough to bury us. Then next season they'll find us all nice and stiff and export us as 'native art'—"

"Were these Llor running from a brush with the Venturi?" Rey wondered. "I thought they were afraid of them. Remember all that trouble about the spy just out of Tharc? We weren't to touch the traders. And even when they found their man the Llor didn't say anything to the caravan people."

"The Llor believe now that they are going to take over Fronn," Kana said. "They must have hated the Venturi for a long time and see a good chance to get back at them now. You scouting tomorrow, Rey?"

"I am—for my sins. And you?"

"Likewise."

Mic nursed his healing arm. "They're sure whittling us

down to size, these mountains. Have bad luck every time
we climb. Fifty lost back there—twenty here—and more
wounded—"

"Not as bad as when the wing bombed us," Rey reminded him. "As long as we can fight back—"

"Yes, I know. But see you come back from scout, you
long-legged byll!"

"You know"—Rey stopped rubbing the snow down his
jaw line—"that's an idea. If a fella could get him say ten-
twenty of those birds and train 'em—as the fur faces
trained their horks. They don't make any noise before
they jump, do they?" He turned to consult Kana as an authority. "No? Well, put 'em on the enemy's track and let
'em go. Better than a Mech crusher in country such as
this."

"And just who is going to catch and train them?" Mic
was beginning, when another Arch appeared out of the
dark.

"Karr?"

"Here!"

"Report to Blademaster."

Kana groped his way to where Hansu had holed up between two overhanging slabs of rock forming a half-cave.
The faint blue of a captured Llor torch gave a ghastly,
morbid hue to the faces of those clustered about it. And
one of them had no face at all—only the blank mask of a
hooded Ventur.

"Karr, sit down." Kana folded up just inside as the
Blademaster turned back to the hooded one.

"Will this man do?"

The muffled head moved, but no word was spoken for a
long moment as Kana shifted under the gaze of eyes hidden behind round holes. Then the trader made an assent-
ing gesture which was more a quick jerk than a Terran
nod.

"This Ventur was a prisoner of that troop of Llor,"
Hansu explained. "He's going back to his people and

you're the AL man who'll accompany him to make contact. We want a base—a chance to hide out until we can notify Secundus. Use your judgment, Karr. You are the only AL trained man we have left. Make the best deal you can with them. Impress upon them that we're as much against the Llor now as they are—tell their leaders what that Corban said to us."

"Yes, sir."

Hansu looked at his watch. "Take rations and extra ammunition. We have no idea how far we now are from Po'ult—the map isn't accurate. And"—he hesitated, his eyes boring into Kana's—"just remember—we have to have that base!"

"Yes, sir."

11

TRUCE OF WIND

The trail ran along a broad ledge from which the snow had
been scoured by the night winds. Below was the dull, dark
green of twisted trees and a gray expanse laced with white
where tempest-driven waves beat upon the water-worn
rocks of the western seashore.

Kana's pace slowed as he looked out over that heaving
floor of water. Winged creatures wheeled, dipped, and
screamed over the narrow strand, seeking out tidbits
thrown up by the flow. But, save for them, he might have
been viewing an empty world.

No sun shone today and under the pewter clouds the
land stretching down to the sea was grim and forbidding.

"We—go—"

Kana started. In all the five hours that they had been
traveling together those were the first words the Ventur
had spoken. Now the trader hovered impatiently at the far
end of the ledge, waiting to climb down to sea level.
Traces on the path marked the retreat of the Llor twenty-
odds hours before. But there were no signs of any Venturi
pursuers.

They had seen no one so far though they had passed

numerous sites intended by nature for easy defense. One might well believe that the traders had no wish to protect their territory.

Now the Combatant toiled down the slope to come out upon a well-marked, smoothly surfaced road along the coast. And within a few minutes they did face a Ventur sentry.

The hooded one who kept watch there conferred with the guide while Kana allowed them the privacy these strange people appeared to desire. He did not join them until the wave of a gloved hand brought him to the small building. Out of this the two traders pushed the first mechanical vehicle the Arch had yet seen on Fronn. It was scarcely more than a platform of metal, possessing three wheels, one at each corner of its wedge shape, and no visible motor. The Ventur guide seated himself on the narrow point and motioned Kana to take his place on the wider section behind. Hardly had the Terran pulled his legs under him than they took off—not at the skimming speed a land jopper would have displayed on his native world— but faster than a marching stride.

As they whisked along he saw no indication of any military patrol. It was as if the Venturi, having driven the Llor into the mountains, no longer worried about an attack, which argued an amazing self-confidence with strength to back it.

The road curved and curled, following the natural contours of the shoreline. They came around one such curve to front the Venturi port.

Here the sea bit into the land in a great semi-circle of a bay, a natural harbor into which the traders had built a series of wharves. Inshore clustered windowless, high-walled buildings with the look of warehouses and trading depots. It was as they approached these that Kana saw the first signs of the recent battle. But all the Venturi in sight were going about their business with no hurry or confusion.

From the odd ships at the wharves—their super-structures completely covered to give them the look of giant turtles —poured a steady stream of goods— Or did it?

The vehicle stopped and Kana got off. No—those ships were being loaded, not unloaded! The flat cars were transporting goods to the sea, not away from it. It was apparent that the traders were stripping the depot—it had all the signs of an orderly evacuation.

"Come—"

Again his Ventur companion hurried him on. They slipped through a maze of lanes between the buildings, hugging the walls at times to avoid swiftly moving cars piled with bundles and bales. And at last they came to a smaller structure so close to the sea that the waters dashed up on its outer wall.

The day without was dull and gray but it was even darker inside the building. Kana blinked, then his wrist was grasped and he was pulled on to the far end of a corridor. As the Ventur stopped before what seemed to be a solid wall, that expanse parted, allowing a greenish light to shine out.

Kana stared about him with a frankness he did not try to disguise. The walls of this room arched over him to meet in a cone's point. Thick pads provided seats for the three Venturi who sat behind low tables. One wall—that to his left—had been covered with a tangle of apparatus which several of the hooded ones were methodically dismantling and packing away in cases. At the entrance of the Terran these stopped their work and slipped out, leaving the Combatant to face the other three.

They had been at work, too, sorting piles of thin sheets of some opaque substance, selecting a few to be encased in a metal chest, tossing others into discard on the floor. Their records, Kana guessed.

The trader who had brought him from the mountains delivered a report. And it was an almost soundless process, as if the Venturi did not communicate by voice alone. When he had done, all the hooded heads swung in Kana's direction. He hesitated, not knowing whether he should speak first. So much depended upon making the right impression. If he could only see their faces—

"You are from off-world?"

It took him a second to decide which one of those baffling masks had addressed him. He thought it was the middle one and replied accordingly.

"I am of Terra—of the Combatants of Terra."

"Why are you here?"

"Skura of the Llor brought us to fight for him. Skura was killed. Now we wish to return to our own world."

"The Llor war—" Was it only his imagination or was there a chill in that voice?

"We no longer fight for the Llor—we fight against them. For they would slay us."

"What seek you of us here?"

"A place to stay until we can find an off-world ship."

"At Tharc are such ships to be found."

"At Tharc are also our enemies. They will not allow us to gain those ships."

"But those at Tharc are also of Terra. Do you war with your own kind?"

"They are evildoers who have broken our laws. They would keep the knowledge of their evil from our Masters-of-Trade. If we can return with the evidence against them, they shall be punished."

"At Tharc only are such ships," repeated the Ventur stubbornly.

"We have heard that near Po'ult is a place where the star ships of off-world traders come," Kana countered with growing desperation. Hansu should have come himself to argue this. He was making no impression at all.

"Traders do not transport men of war—traders do not fight."

"But we met Llor in the mountains fleeing from a battle with traders—traders they no longer welcome in the plains. No, Master-of-Trade—the hour is coming when even you may be forced to bare sword and use rifle in your own defense. We spoke with a Llor Corban who foretold the sacking of your mainland holdings—of a new day coming to Fronn when the Venturi would not rule the caravan routes. Those who would press this change upon you are prepared to do it with the sword. And they are also *our* enemies. We are fighting men, trained to battle from our earliest years. Those whom our swords serve sleep easy at night. And it seems that you will have need of allies, Master, if rumor speaks true."

The hooded figure changed position slightly, almost as if he had answered that with a shrug.

"We be of the sea. And the Llor are not of the sea. If we keep to our own place, what need have we of swords? And soon enough the dwellers on land will come to know their mistake."

"If you dealt only with Llor, perhaps that would be true. But the Llor have these others to aid them. The renegade Terrans they company do not fight as we do, rifle to rifle, sword to sword. Rather do they have mighty machines to obey their will and they hunt from the sky, raining fire upon those they would destroy. To passage through the air the sea is no barrier. Tell me, Master, are there not off-world men who would be glad if your hold upon the trade of Fronn ceased to be? Such men will give support in war to those who serve them best."

When they did not have a ready answer to that a tiny spark of hope came to Kana. If the Venturi were deserting their shore bases, preparing to withdraw to their island fortresses for an indefinite length of time, then the Horde might reach the sea coast only to discover themselves in another trap. His chance—their only chance—was to win at least grudging support from these traders before they departed.

"These things of which you speak have already been told to us. The sky machines have been sighted. So you think they would follow us—even into the outer ocean where no Llor dares to drive a ship?"

"I believe this, Master-of-Trade, that peace has departed from Fronn and that the time has come when all upon its surface will be compelled to choose whether they shall follow this war leader or that. It was against the law that these sky fighters and moving fortresses were brought here. And when men go outside the law—a law which has might to back it—they do so weighing risk against return —as you in trade weigh risk against profit. They play now to rule this world. And if they win—what will they care for the Venturi? You shall be eaten up and your trade kingdom shall be as if it never was!"

The middle Ventur arose, his robes making a faint whispering as he moved, for they were of a finer material than the drab coverings of the caravan men.

"We are not of those who make treaties or deal with rulers," he stated firmly, "but the words you have spoken shall be carried to our elders on Po'ult. And to this much shall we agree—you may bring your people to this—the Landing of Po'ult—and they may abide here through the great storms—until our elders come to a decision, for we shall be gone from here this day. This is spoken by Falt'u'th, so be it recorded."

A murmur from the others gave assent. The guide who had brought Kana waved him to withdraw. He brought his hand up in salute and the Venturi leader nodded. As the Terran left the room the men who had been dismantling the machine on the wall hurried past him to resume their work.

Venturi hospitality was not expansive. Kana was transported from the Landing of Po'ult at once. As the wedge car ascended the slope behind the settlement he noticed one of the turtle ships drawing away from the dock. As it neared the middle of the bay it slowly submerged until only a conning tower was left above water, and with that cutting the waves it headed to the open sea.

Kana and the Ventur reached the guard post at dusk and the Terran was thankful to note that the trader intended to spend the night there. The Combatant was shown into a windowless inner room, one wall of which gave off a faint greenish gleam, provided with a mat which could be either seat or bed, and left to himself. He ate his rations and curled up on the pad, aching with weariness.

The next morning it was made clear to him that the Venturi regarded this outpost as the boundary of their concern with him and from that point he was to proceed alone. But now the pale sun was banishing the gloom of the day before and, as he swung along at the ground-eating pace of the marching Arch, his confidence in the future grew. After all—even if the traders had not opened Po'ult, they were allowing the Terrans the use of their port on the coast. And it was situated not far from the landing field Hansu had spoken of—they had only to await the coming of an off-world trading ship.

Kana's hopeful outlook continued to grow as he climbed the pass, and it colored the report he was able to make to Hansu before noon.

"They gave you no idea as to when they would let us know their decision?" The Blademaster pinned him down.

"No, sir. They were stripping the Landing, withdrawing to their sea strongholds. Seemed to think that they could outsit the trouble—"

"I have yet to see a neutral win anything—especially when the enemy wants something he has. But we can't quarrel with even half luck—we'll settle for the use of their port buildings now."

When the van of the Horde reached the outer guard post they found it deserted, the building empty, the sentry and the wedge car gone. And as they marched on down to the Landing nothing moved in the narrow lanes between the warehouses. The turtle ships had vanished—a last conning tower slicing the waves could just be seen far out on the bay. But not a Ventur, not a scrap of their goods was left in the silent and empty port.

Hansu posted sentries, though he allowed that the sturdiness of the thick walls would be ample protection against the most that even a Mech force could throw against them. The Blademaster took up quarters in the house backing upon the sea where Kana had met with the Venturi leaders. The apparatus was gone from the wall of the room, leaving holes and dangling brackets, but the small tables were still bolted to the floor and a seat pad had been left behind.

For the first time since they had left Tharc the Combatants were under roofs. And none too soon, for the rising wind of the night brought with it the banners of a storm.

The thick walls kept out most of the howl of the wind. But one could lay a hand against their surfaces and feel the vibration of such tempests as the Terrans had not known before. They need fear no attack while this held.

Curiosity led them to explore their new quarters, finding a few discarded articles, the use of half of which they could not deduce. Kana, with Mic and Rey, armed with Terran night torches, dared a trap door they discovered in a far hallway and descended a steep flight of steps whose risers had not been fashioned for off-world feet. They ended in a cellar, half natural sea cave, in which a water-filled slip ran part way up, slopping back and forth with the force of the wind-driven sea without.

Flicking his light across the water Kana sighted a line fastened inconspicuously to a hook embedded in the floor, pulled taut below the surface. Something heavy must be tethered there!

He gave it a questioning tug. There was an object on the other end all right. The three of them dragged it together, bracing their feet and trying to free what lay below with a series of sharp jerks. Seconds later they pulled up the slimy incline a strange craft. It was rounded, contained, like the turtle ships—more so, for it lacked the conning tower.

"A bomb?" ventured Mic.

"No, not when it's anchored that way." Kana moved around the end. "One man escape ship maybe."

"They went off and forgot it—?"

"No," Kana denied again. "It was hidden—so I'd say we still have a visitor."

"Left behind to watch us—" Mic's eyes roved about the rough walls. "Perhaps he's to set some traps, too."

"I don't think that the Venturi have the trap-type mind," Kana defended the traders. "I'd say we were left an observer—maybe even a contact with Po'ult, if we handle it right. However, perhaps it would be better if we kept a watch on this." He kicked the ship with the toe of his boot. Whoever traveled in that would have cramped quarters indeed. A Terran could not fit in it at all, not even when flat and unmoving.

They reported the find to Hansu and the ship was transported to an upper hall. A searching exploration was made of all the Landing buildings without any concrete results.

The storm had not blown out by morning. Instead it increased and it became almost impossible, because of the wind and driven spray, to win from one building to another. But this would continue to keep off attack—which almost balanced the Arch disappointment at being unable to search for the space port Hansu was sure must be close at hand.

Kosti examined the escape ship with care and solved the riddle of its opening, displaying to his crowding comrades the narrow padded slit within, which would cradle the body of the navigator.

"What kinda man would fit in there?" demanded Sim.

"Perhaps not a 'man' at all," Kosti returned.

"Huh?"

"Well, none of us have seen a Ventur without one of those muffling robes. How do we know if they are like the

Llor—or us? This could be comfortable for a non-human."

Kana eyed the slit speculatively. It was too narrow for the length if it were fashioned to accommodate a humanoid. It suggested an extremely thin, sinuous creature. He did not feel any prick of man's age-old distaste for the reptilian—any reminder of the barrier between warm-blooded and cold-blooded life which had once held on his home world. Racial mixtures after planet-wide wars, mutant births after the atomic conflicts, had broken down the old intolerance against the "different." And out in space thousands of intelligent life forms, encased in almost as many shapes and bodies, had given "shape prejudice" its final blow. The furred Llor and Cos were "man"-shaped, but it might be that they shared Fronn with another race, evolved from scaled clans.

Why not snake or lizard? There were races whose far ancestors had been feline, and others who had, dim ages ago, sacrificed the wings of birds to develop intelligence and civilization—and yet the Yabanu and the Trystian were now equal partners in the space lanes. As for reptiles —what of the lizard Zacathans, whose superior learning had confounded half the universe and yet who were a most peace-loving and law-abiding collection of scholars?

Kana, remembering the Zacathans he had known and admired, viewed that padded cushion with no aversion, only curiosity. What did it matter if a body was covered with wool, or with scales, or with soft flesh which had to be protected by clothing? The Venturi he had met had not been in any way terrifying or obnoxious creatures—once one became used to their constant concealment of their faces and forms. Now he wanted to know what they were really like—and why they shrouded themselves so carefully.

But the owner of the escape ship, if he were concealed somewhere within the Landing, made no move to declare his presence. And the storm continued. On the morning of

the second day Hansu fought his way across a short strip
of court to a nearby building and returned, being once
hurled against a wall with a force which almost lost him
his footing. Kana, waiting, grabbed for the Blademaster's
coat and dragged him inside. The commander gasped
painfully before he could speak.

"We can't face this. It is the West Wind Drive!"

Kana recalled the record-pak. The West Wind Drive,
that paralyzing push of Fronn's terrible windy season
when all life went to cover and death itself rode the blasts.
There would be no hope of surviving even a short journey
in the open. Anything caught outside the shelter of the
Landing would be whirled off and battered flat. Their luck
had held—bringing them out of the mountains behind the
strong walls of the port just in time.

"No spacer would try to land now," Kana pointed out.
"They would be warned."

Hansu nodded. But it was plain that his inability to do
something about the situation was an added irritant.

"I wish I could meet that Ventur." He gazed down the
hall as if he could summon the hidden one out by the force
of his will. "We must be ready to move the minute this
clears."

Their future was still a race for time. If the Blademaster
could get a messenger aboard a spacer before Hart Device
located them and brought up his wings—they would win.
And—did the Venturi hold the deciding cards in this
game?

12

ON TO PO'ULT

The inactivity caused by the storms began to bore the Combatants. At first they had been content to sleep much of the time, rebuilding the stores of energy worn out by the trek across the mountains. But now they roamed restlessly through the buildings, making reckless sorties from one to another during what they believed were lulls, or allowed their irritation to show in sudden snarling quarrels. But Hansu was prepared to meet this. There were drilling in unarmed combat and scouting, follow-the-leader hunts in which a handful of veterans hid and the younger members of the teams traced them in silent pursuit.

Since the storm established a perpetual gray dusk one could no longer distinguish day from night. It might have been noon or well into evening when Kana climbed one of the perilously steep flights of narrow stairs to almost roof level of a warehouse. His eyes had long since adjusted to the pallid green light given off by the walls and he moved softly, intent upon reaching the small platform just under the curve of the domed roof. From there he would be able to see into the large storage space which occupied the center section of the building. He was a hound and Sim was hare today. It had become a matter of pride for the recruit to locate this one veteran, even if he must devote every moment until the sleep period to the problem.

As Kana climbed, the light faded. He put out a hand to touch the steps as a guide. But he was still at least three from the top when he stopped and shrank against the wall. He sensed that he was not alone.

From below he had estimated that the platform was about five feet square. There was a trap door above it which must give upon the roof—and in this wind nothing could perch outside for an instant. The roof!

Kana's shoulder rubbed the wall as he forced his memory to reconstruct the outline of this warehouse building as he had seen it from the headquarters two hours before. It was, like all the rest, a rounded dome which offered small resistance to the wind. The roof—

He took the remaining steps cautiously. Then he stretched to his full height, raising his arms above his head until his fingers were on the surface above him. But what he expected he did not find.

Twice during these scout games he had climbed to these vantage points in warehouses and both times he had discovered that the roof vibrated faintly, a trembling born of the blasts beating across it. But here it was quiet, as if insulated against the outer world. And he still believed that he was not alone.

With his finger tips he explored the ceiling, locating the small trap door which should give on the roof. As his hands fingered its hinges he realized that here was a difference. There was no fastening on this side. The latch which kept the door from swinging down must be on the other side!

Kana slipped his torch from his belt and snapped it on at the lowest power, no longer caring if Sim sighted him. The platform was covered by that gritty dust which constantly sifted through the air during the storms. His boots had left plain tracks in it. But there were other marks too, though these were shapeless scuffs which could not have been left by a Terran unless he had purposely tried to conceal his spoor. And directly under the trap door were other marks he could not identify.

He beamed the torch up at the door. It was firmly set; he could hardly see the lines marking the square. The two hinges glistened. Kana investigated delicately. Grease—some sort of grease so recently applied that it was liquid instead of viscid and its strange odor was sharp as he brought his smeared finger to his nose. Someone was using this door. But to go outside—that was impossible!

Kana aimed the beam at the ceiling, beginning his examination farther out than the platform. After a careful study he was certain that there was a space overhead between the ceiling he saw and the outer dome of the building. The curve was curtailed, the angle between the side wall and the dome sharper than it should be. But what a perfect hiding place! No Terran would attempt to explore the roofs in the storm. He was prepared to take Knife-Oath that he had discovered the hiding place of the Venturi spy! Hansu need only station a guard here and—

A whisper of sound, so faint it barely reached his ears, made him snap off the torch and back against the wall to the left of the stairs. Some of the green radiance seeped up, but the light was so faint he could not really see. He must depend upon his ears—his nose.

For now he was aware of an odor. Below, where the bales of trade goods had once been stored, smells fought with one another and the general aroma was often sickening to a Terran. But this was different, faintly spicy and fresh—transporting him for an instant to the gambling establishment on Secundus. There was nothing unpleasant about it and it was growing stronger.

Next came a soft plop and Kana froze, hardly daring to breathe. Something, his ears told him, had fallen from the trap door to the platform. He swung his torch before him as if it were a flamer.

Other sounds reached him—movements he was not sure of.

He pressed the stud of the torch, setting the power at full. And it flashed on, pinning in its thick beam the creature who had just stepped from the last loop in a rope ladder to the floor. It made one grab for the rope and then froze, erect and quiet, accepting the fact that escape was now impossible.

The cushioned bed in the escape ship had been a clue right enough, but reality out-stripped imagination. If this were a Ventur—and Kana had no reason to doubt that—the second major race of Fronn had little or nothing in common with the Llor physically.

Its extreme slenderness gave it the appearance of greater height than it really possessed, for it was shorter than he. Its arms fitted to the barrel of the trunk without any width of shoulder and the pouchy neck was only a shade under the girth of the chest. The legs were long and as thin as a gu's ending in flat, webbed feet, and there were two sets of upper limbs, all equipped with six-fingered hands.

But the head was the least humanoid, four eyes set in pairs on either side, a wide mouth which now gaped in surprise, no visible chin— Kana started as with horror he realized where he had seen the like before—in miniature. This was a tif—a tif turned land dweller with only its size and greater brain case to distinguish it from the ferocious hunters of the river.

As Kana remembered the tif he knew the cold chill of fear—until he met those eyes blinking in the torture of his light. The black beads of hate, promising all manner of evil to come, which had watched him from the stream were not here. These larger orbs were golden, intelligent, mildly peaceful. And the Arch guessed that the Ventur was as alarmed as he—tif the other might look, but tif in nature he was not.

None of those four hands had gone to the knife which

was sheathed on the Ventur's hip. A shiver crossed the green-gray skin beneath the scanty tunic which covered it to mid-thigh. Abruptly Kana switched off the torch.

And then it was his turn to blink as a green beam, far under the power of his own, struck him, flitting from head to boots and back again.

"One only?" The question out of the dark did not sound as if it had come from between those wide loose lips, out of the wattled throat.

"Just one."

The light went to his hands and then to his sword-knife at his belt. It centered there for a moment as if the Ventur was studying the weapon—as if that undrawn blade answered some private question for the other.

"You will come?" The green light pinpointed the dangling ladder.

Kana did not hesitate. He thrust his own torch back in its loop and stepped forward.

He made the short climb up the rope and wedged his shoulders through the trap door. It was a tight fit. Above was a pocket-sized room. A spongy pad covered a third of the space and he sat down on one end of it as his host emerged from the floor and made some adjustment which brought more light from the walls. There was, in addition to the pad, a flat box and a neat pile of containers. By the end of the cushion was a small brazier emitting coils of spicy, scented smoke. The quarters might be cramped, but the hidy-hole was provided with Venturi comforts. And now the frog-man seated himself on the other end of the pad, pushing aside his folded robe.

"You have watched us?" Kana asked.

"I have watched you." The ungainly head, its four golden eyes fixed on the Terran, gave a twitch of agreement.

"For the Masters-of-Trade?"

"For the nation," the other corrected swiftly. "You are traders in death. Such bargains may be evil—"

"You are a speaker-for-many?"

"I train to be a speaker-for-many. I am but one of limited years and small wisdom. You are a lord over many swords?"

It was Kana's turn to deny honors. "I, too, am but a learner of this trade. This is my first battle journey."

"Tell me, why do you creep through these buildings spying upon one another?" the Ventur asked, a note of real puzzlement in his voice.

"We train ourselves—that we may come upon the enemy secretly. It is a practice of our art."

The four eyes continued to regard him unblinkingly. "And the Llor is now this enemy you would creep upon unseen. But why—did not the Llor summon you to Fronn in their service? Why should you now turn against them?"

"We were brought to serve the Chortha Skura. He made a bargain with our Masters-of-Trade. But he was killed in the first battle. According to custom we then ceased from battle and asked to be returned to our own place. But the Llor invited our Masters to hold a meeting over this matter, and when they were gathered together the Llor killed them treacherously. It was then that we discovered that they had with them certain outlaws of our own kind whose desire was to hunt us all down lest we return to our Masters-of-Trade and report the truth of what was done. Now our enemies hold Tharc where our space ships land. We came to Po'ult hoping to find a trading spacer that would carry a messenger off-world for us—"

"But those which land here are not ships of war."

"It does not matter whether they are or not. They are not so small that they have not space for one or two men besides their crew. And once our Masters-of-Trade know what has happened they will send ships to take us off."

"Then you do not wish to stay on Fronn? With such arts of war as you know you might win the leadership of this world."

"We are of Terra. To us that is the world to call home. All we wish is to leave Fronn in peace."

The Ventur leaned forward to draw in deep breaths of the smoke arising from the brazier. Then, without a word, he opened a round box and brought out two small basins or handleless cups. They were fashioned in the form of spiraled shells of a delicate blue-green across which moved amethyst shadows. Into each of these he measured a minute portion of golden liquid poured from a small flagon as beautifully made as the cups. Then he held out one to Kana while he lifted the other, chanting some words in his own tongue.

Kana accepted the cups gingerly. He could not refuse to drink—it was offered with too much ceremony, though what effect the native liquor might have on a Terran stomach and head worried him, even as the stuff slid smoothly over his tongue and he swallowed. There was no sensation of heat such as Terran strong drink brought—only a coolness, a tingling which spread outward to the tips of his fingers and the surface of his skin. He set down the empty cup. Now what he sensed was mingled in some odd way with the scent from the brazier and the green radiance of the walls, as if taste, touch, smell and sight were suddenly one, all the keener and sharper for that uniting.

The Ventur shrugged his robe into place about his shoulders.

"We go now to your Master-of-Swords—"

Did he hear those words with his ears, mused Kana, or did they ring in his mind only? He stood up, this strange clarity of the senses persisting, and watched the frog-man drop the rope into the darkness below the trap door. On the platform the Ventur paused to adjust his hood, hiding his strange face.

"He's in the other building," Kana warned, remembering the storm.

"Yes—" The robed shadow glided noiselessly along, al-

most entirely invisible to anyone who did not know where
he was. Kana knew that that must have protected him as
he spied upon the Combatants.

They covered the few feet between the door of the
warehouse and the recessed entrance of headquarters
clinging to one another and both Kana's coat and the
skirts of the other's robe were soaked with sea spray as
they won to their goal.

Not only were his senses more acute, Kana decided, but
his reactions were swifter. He was conscious of so much
he had not noted before—that there were subtle differ-
ences in the shades of green light from room to room—
that sounds hitherto drowned out by the muffled roar of
the wind were perceptible.

"What's that—!" A Swordsman coming down the hall
halted at the sight of the Ventur.

"Messenger to Hansu," Kana explained, hurrying his
companion on to meet the Blademaster.

Hansu and two of the Swordtans glanced up frowning at
the interruption. But they were alert at the sight of the
trader.

"Where did you—?" the Blademaster began and then
addressed the silent Ventur. "What is it that you wish?"

"It is rather what you wish, Master-of-Swords," the
other returned. "You desire a meeting with our Masters-
of-Trade. But I have not the right to answer in their name.
This one of you"—the cowled head gave a half turn to in-
dicate Kana—"has made clear to me why you are here
and what you wish. Grant me"—he mentioned a space of
Fronnian time—"and I shall have an answer for you."

Hansu did not hesitate. "Done! But how can you communicate with your people? In this storm—"

Kana received a vivid impression of the Ventur's
amusement. "Do you then have no means among you of
talking across distances, Terran? We have been rated a
backward people by off-world races, but we have not displayed all our knowledge and resources before them.

Come with me if you wish and see. There is no trickery in what I would do, only the use of things built by intelligent beings for their safety and comfort."

So it was that Kana and Hansu returned to that hidden room to watch the Ventur, his hampering robe discarded, open a thin box and display a silver mirror disc and a row of small levers. These he raised or lowered in a pattern, with infinite care, as if he worked out a complicated combination.

The mirror misted and at the coming of that film the Ventur moved quickly to snatch up a slender rod. With the pointed tip of that he traced a series of waving lines. They faded from the disc and there was a moment of waiting until the mist reappeared and a second collection of lines were inscribed. Four times that happened and then the trader put aside his pen.

"There is a matter of time now," he informed the Combatants. "We must wait until the Masters reply. I only report, it is for them to give orders."

Hansu grunted. There were cruel lines of weariness about the Blademaster's mouth, a cloud of fatigue in his eyes. Hansu was a man worn close to the edge of endurance. And what ate into him was not only the future of the Horde—but something even more important. He was fighting for more than their escape from Fronn—for a goal which might be of far greater importance than the lives of all the Archs on this world.

The Ventur inhaled the brazier smoke, but his golden eyes watched the Terrans.

"Master," he said to the Blademaster, "this much I can tell you—there has not been any off-world ship land here for ten tens of clors—"

Kana tried to translate the time measure. Close to four months' ship time! His mouth set hard.

"And that is not as it was in the past?"

"It is not," the Blademaster was answered. "We do not care for off-world trade, so its lack did not disturb us. But now—perhaps you can read another meaning into this. Also, what can you do if the trade ship comes not? Your enemies hold the port at Tharc."

"One thing at a time. Let me speak to your Masters and then we shall see—"

A tinkle of sound came from the box. The Ventur looked at the mirror. Although the Terrans could make nothing of what he saw there he spoke in a moment or two.

"The Masters summon you to Po'ult to speak with them in private council. And because you have met with treachery on Fronn, there shall be those of master rank who shall sit among your men as hostages while you are gone. To this do you agree?"

"I agree. But when do I go?"

"The first fury of the storm will ebb tonight. They will send a ship in, but you must be ready to return with it at once, for this lull will not last long."

"Am I to go alone?"

"Take one man if you wish. May I suggest this one." A claw finger pointed at Kana. "He speaks the trade tongue well."

Hansu did not object. "Let it be so."

The lull came as the Ventur had foretold. And the two Terrans went with the trader down the sea-slimed steps to the dock. Kana saw the vee of spray cutting down the bay, heralding the approach of a Venturi vessel. It arose from the water and came in to the pier with perfection of handling. Then a hatch in the conning tower opened and four robed figures disembarked. Three glided up to the Terrans, the other remained by the ship.

"This Master Roo'uf, Under-Master Rs'ad, and Under-Master Rr'ol—they shall stay with your men."

Hansu escorted the Venturi back to introduce them to his Swordtans. Then, with Kana at his heels, he climbed the ladder leading to the hatch. Within was a second ladder dropping into green dimness and the Combatants descended while strange odors and stranger noises closed about them as they went. The Ventur spy touched Kana's sleeve and drew him to the left.

"It is the thought of the master of this ship that you would be interested in watching from the lookout as we travel— This way."

They squeezed along a passage which was almost too narrow to accommodate Terrans and found themselves in a circular space where a wide seat pad ran three-quarters of the way around, broken only by the door through which they had entered. Directly facing them was a section of what appeared to be transparent glass. And beyond that they could see the clustered buildings of the Landing.

A Ventur without a robe was seated on the pad watching the scene intently. He gave them only a casual gesture of greeting before the dock began to recede and the whole shore line whipped to the right as the ship turned. The voyage to Po'ult had begun.

13

LIFE OR DEATH TRADE

Po'ult rose out of the sea abruptly—the toothed rock walls of the island's rim lifting vertically from the sea without any softening fringe of beach. And on the crest of those walls there were no signs of buildings.

Having afforded its passengers a single good look at the island the ship submerged until even the conning tower was under water. The Terrans were led down close to the keel, to wedge themselves into a smaller craft with two of the Venturi. Vibration sang in the walls of that tiny boat but there was no other indication that they had left the parent vessel.

Kana tensed. The sensation of being confined far below the surface of the sea oppressed him. But their voyage did not last long and when the hatch was raised they were in an underground port, a large-scale copy of the subcellar landing place back on the continent.

They saw but little of the Venturi city, being taken along passages chiseled through the native rock to a room near the top of the cliff, one side of which was transparent. Their guide withdrew and Kana went over to that window, craving the feeling of freedom it gave.

"Volcano crater," Hansu observed.

The center of the island was a cup, its walls terraced and planted, a grove of trees extending into a miniature woodland in the depth of the hollow. But there were no signs of buildings.

"But where—"

The Blademaster looked beyond the peaceful carpet of vegetation to the crater walls.

"We're in their city now," he explained. "They've hollowed out the cliffs—"

In a moment Kana saw the evidences of that—the regular openings in the rock which must equal such windows as the one before which he now stood.

"What a scheme!" he marveled. "Even a bomber would have a hard time putting this out of commission—unless it dropped hot stuff—"

At the corner of the Blademaster's jaw a tiny muscle pulled tight.

"When the law is broken once, it can be easily fractured again."

"Use hot stuff?" Kana's horrified amazement was genuine. He could accept the enmity of the Mechs, even the struggle for power backed in some mysterious way by Central Control Agents, but the thought of turning to atomics for weapons against—! Terra had learned too bitter a lesson in the Big Blow-up and the wars which followed. Those had occurred a thousand years ago but they had scarred the memories of his species for all time. He could not conceive of a Terran using an atomic weapon—it was so unnatural that it made his head reel.

"We've had evidence enough that this is not just a Mech plot," Hansu pointed out relentlessly. "We may be conditioned against hot stuff because of our past history—but others aren't. And we daren't overlook any possibility—"

That was an axiom of the corps he should have remembered. Never overlook any possibility, be prepared for any change in prospects—in the balance of force against force.

"War Lord"—one of the frog people had come up silently behind them—"the Masters would speak with you."

No hospitality had been offered them before that meeting, Kana noted, disturbed, no gesture made which could be termed friendly. He fell a step behind the Blademaster and stood at attention as they entered a room where four Venturi, their robes laid aside, awaited them.

The soft fabric of their short tunics was a somber blue-purple and there were gems set in their belts and in the broad bracelets they wore encircling all four upper limbs. At some distance squatted a fifth, writing pen in one hand and a block of the mirror stuff on the floor before him.

A single seat pad was placed facing the court and Hansu took his seat there, Kana standing behind him.

"We have been informed of what you wish." The Ventur whose tunic boasted a symbol stitched upon its breast opened the meeting without ceremony. "You wish a place of refuge for your men until you can make contact with your superiors off-world. Why should we be interested in what happens to interlopers, introduced on Fronn through no fault of ours? And since you are now being hunted by the Llor and these new allies of theirs, it might mean that in giving you sanctuary we would bring upon us the wrath of those at Tharc."

"Does not a state of war already exist between you and Tharc?" countered Hansu. "When we crossed the mountains we were met by a party of Llor driven off from an attack on the Landing. From them we rescued one of your men."

The frog-man's broad face displayed no emotion the Terrans could read.

"The Venturi do not war, they trade. And when it is not time to trade, when the world is disturbed, we withdraw until the mainland is sane again. So has it been in the past and that system has always worked to our advantage."

"But before did the Llor ever have allied with them

those who could bring war through the air? Perhaps Po'ult cannot be captured from the sea—but what if you are attacked from above, Master of Many Ships?"

"*You* have no machine which can ride the wind, are these others then more powerful than you?"

"They are ones who have been trained in a different mode of making war. And it is against our custom for them to use that warfare upon such a world as Fronn. With the weapons they have they can make themselves master of this whole planet if they wish. Do you think that your withdrawal will avail you if that is their plan? One by one they shall search out your island strongholds and rain destruction upon you from the air. They may even bring to subdue you the burning death—which is a weapon forbidden to all living creatures—a weapon so terrible that its use once wrecked my own world and sent my race back to barbarism for centuries. For"—Hansu repeated the warning he had voiced to Kana earlier—"when the law is once broken, it is easily fractured again. These renegades have broken our law by coming to Fronn, and from that they may go on to worse things—"

"If you do not fight as do these others, then why or how could you be of service to us?"

"Just this—" Hansu held himself stiffly erect, braced as if facing an enemy charge. "The news of what has occurred here must be carried to our first rank Masters. Only they have the power to deal with these outlaws. And that message must be carried by one to whom they will listen. Give my men refuge and I, myself, will take the message off-world. And I promise you that when I am heard by our inner Council there shall be a reckoning and Fronn shall be cleansed. So that here off-world men shall be forbidden to land—as has happened on other planets—and you shall be left to manage your affairs as you wish. Do you not know that there are those who do not wish to see

the trade of Fronn only Venturi trade? They would help
the Llor to break you as they would a rotten stick for a
night campfire—for the Llor are ignorant of the mysteries
of your craft and those from off-world would speedily take
it all into their own hands—to hold forever! You have
never welcomed the alien traders and they would be free
of your restrictions."

Was the Blademaster making an impression? Kana
could not tell. And his hopes sank when the spokesman of
the Masters answered:

"You say much which we must consider in council. Be
thou becalmed in our waters this night—"

That last had the flavor of some formula of hospitality.
And the Terrans discovered that it meant escort to a room
overlooking the valley where two of the treasured smoke
braziers filled the air with spicy scent. One of the Masters
came in, followed by a lesser trader bearing a tray on
which were set out three cups and a ewer. The Master
poured out a small measure of the same liquid Kana had
been given in the hidden room, and proffered the cups to
the Combatants with his own hands. Again Kana sipped
the icy stuff and felt it seep through him, bringing once
more the heightened senses, the alertness of mind and
body. The ceremonial drink was borne away and small tables set up on which were laid a series of dishes, none containing more than a mouthful or so of that particular
viand.

"These foods have been exported off-world," the Master assured them. "They can be safely eaten by those of
your species."

The Terrans ate, thankful for the change from rations,
finding the subtle flavors intriguing. The Venturi were art-
ists in food, striving for strange effects—substances were
hot and cold at the same time, a sharp sour was followed
by a bland sweet, the whole blending into a feeling of gas-
tronomic content such as Kana, for one, had never before
experienced.

"Your city is well concealed." Hansu gestured toward the bucolic scene in the crater valley.

"The plan was not intended to conceal," corrected the Master. "When our far-off ancestors first crawled from water to land they lived in caves within the cliffs of these sea islands. So, instead of building in the open, our race built within the land—for it is our nature to wish our living space to be enclosed and close to water. As our intelligence and civilization grew our cities became such as Po'ult. We are uncomfortable on the dry plains of the large continents—each of us must serve his apprenticeship there as a duty but he is joyful when he may return to his home island. Are you of a race which lives in the open as do the Llor?"

Hansu nodded, and began to describe Terra, her blue skies, green hills, and open, changeable seas.

"Tell me, since you appear to be one who thinks upon matters beyond his duties for the day, why do you sell your skill to war? You are not barbarian as are the Llor, who are a young race. You must come of an old people, perhaps older than we. Why have you not realized that what you do is a waste, a negation of growth and good?"

"We are born with a will to struggle, a desire to match our strength against that of others. Among our kind when that inner urge is stilled the tribe or nation which has lost it declines. We broke into outer space—and that was a struggle and goal which absorbed us for centuries—we were eager for the stars. But we discovered that space was not ours—that there we were deemed as young and barbaric as the Llor. There were many races and species before us and they had fashioned a code of law and order to control newcomers. Those who exercised that control judged us and ruled that we were, because of our temperaments, unfit for space except within the boundaries they set. Since it was in our nature to fight, we were to provide the mercenaries for other planets. We were geared to that service, a small piece fitted into *their* pattern. And so it is with us—the price we must pay for the stars since there is this guard upon the stellar lanes."

"To me that does not sound like an equal bargain," commented their host. "And when any bargain is uneven, there comes a day when it will be declared no bargain and he who has been defrauded will go elsewhere to trade. Does the time come when you of Terra will go elsewhere?"

"Perhaps. And what happens here on Fronn may decide that."

"May your trading be even, the profit good!"

"May your ships ever return filled from far voyaging." Hansu made the proper answer as the Master left them.

The Combatants were not summoned to attend the Masters again that day. Soon the storm closed in for a second prolonged buffeting and the window through which they watched the crater was obscured most of the time by foam and flying debris caught up by the gusts.

"D'you think we have a chance?" Kana ventured to interrupt the silence as Hansu stared into the wildness without.

"At least they are now giving us the attention due honored guests. When they fed us they acknowledged equality. And when you win one point you have advanced that far. But their logic is not ours. We cannot deduce what they are going to do by what we would do in their place. You, as an AL man should know that. This *is* your first enlistment?"

"Yes, sir."

"Why did you try for AL rating?"

"I liked the basic course, sir. There was a Zacathan instructor—he made me think a lot. And the way his mind worked fascinated me. Through him I met other X-Tees. So I signed for specialization testing and I passed the prelim. It isn't too popular a course—too many extra hours. But—well, sir—it never seemed really like work to me. And visiting around in the X-Tee quarters was more inter-

esting than taking town leave—at least I liked it better
though we weren't encouraged to—"

"Make off-world friends, no. Just to learn the minimum
enabling us to get around on other planets—*I* know!"
Hansu interrupted. "Of course to Central Control we're
the oddest beasts of all."

"Deke said something like that once, sir," mused Kana.
"That Central Control had a mental picture of us and it
was so well established that they didn't see the real Terrans at all—"

"Mills knew what he was talking about. We're breaking
law and custom right now—daring to treat with these
Venturi on our own. And it's about time we did more of
this."

When Kana curled up on the pads for sleep he left the
Blademaster still brooding by the window. Outside the
night was a black whirlwind but here the roar was the
faintest of murmurs.

In the morning they were shown a bathing place with a
pool of sea water deep enough for swimming. And after-
ward they dined again lavishly. Their visit with the council
did not come until mid-morning.

"We have considered this problem," the foremost Master began when the Blademaster had taken his seat, "and
your argument has within it many points with which we
must agree. However, the future is always chance. We
cannot transport your men here, our economy is a tight
one, our space limited—we could not house such a number of off-world beings for an indefinite period. We cannot, in fact, use sea transport at all, except for short intervals, until the peak storms of this season are over. But
then, neither can your enemy move against you. Therefore
you have about ten dytils in which to study the situation
and make your plans. At the end of that time, if you can
see a chance to get off-world with your message, we agree
to transport your men, not here to Po'ult, but to a larger
island south of here, farther asea, on which we pasture our

caravan guen during the stormy season. We will under-
take, moreover, to supply your men with food and instructions in the art of netting such sea creatures as they may
safely devour."

"And in return you ask of us?"

"And in return we ask your word that you will speak
with your Masters so that off-world men be forbidden to
land on Fronn to fight our battles. And that those who
may come be granted that right only after the Venturi has
had their application and know the purpose for which they
wish to visit us. We do not wish Fronn to become tributary
to another world, or be possessed by some trading com-
bine of distant stars."

"To this I agree, not only as a bargain, but because it is
what I believe myself," Hansu retorted. "We return now
to the Landing?"

"Within two light periods of this dytil there will be a
second lull. Then you shall return, and with you one of
our Those-who-talk-for-many to be a link with us across
the distance. Fair winds and a good profit to you, Lord of
Many Swords."

"And to you, Master of Ten Thousand Ships, a smooth
sea."

The lull which gave opportunity for their return to the
Landing came at last and was longer than the previous
one. In fact, the calm continued so long after their arrival
on the main continent that, had it not been for the advice
of the Ventur communications expert, the Terrans might
have made the mistake of trying to reach the space field.
But his warning kept them close to the buildings and the
predictions he made were fulfilled when a scream arose
out of the dark, whistling above the thud of waves on the
shore—the opening cry of a new storm.

"We have received no off-world signals from any star
ship." The Ventur sipped at a drink made from Terran ration pellets dissolved in water. "It is the belief of the Masters that none may planet here again. Why should they? If

Tharc is now open to their use and the Llor encourage them to think that in the future they shall not have to deal with us—why then should they come here?"

"True enough." Hansu swallowed the warm broth.

"And if there is no chance of finding a ship here, you will make other plans?"

"We may have to go to Tharc."

The frog-man had no eyebrows to raise, but he did radiate polite incredulity. Only courtesy kept him from asking how that was to be done. But Hansu did not volunteer any explanation.

The storm did not last as long as the previous one and Kana knew that the series of such strong blows was now on the wane. It was noon on the following day when the Ventur announced that it was safe to go into the open. The Combatants were eager to get out, to draw the chill fresh salt air into their lungs and poke about in the curious rubbish the winds had piled against corners of the warehouse courts.

A shout from the farthest-ranging exploring party brought all those within earshot. Jammed at a crazy angle between outlying buildings, where none of the Horde had been stationed, was the mashed wreckage of a machine— looking as if some giant had caught it up and wrung it around as a man might a wet under-tunic.

"A crawler—that's a crawler!" the awed voice of its discoverer repeated. And, while no one disputed him, they could hardly believe the evidence of their own eyes.

A crawler—not as large as a land fortress certainly, but in its way as formidable a piece of mechanized war machinery—to be so mangled and tossed here as if it were constructed of straw.

The outer hatch was open, forced straight up by the impact, and now Kosti climbed up the battered metal shell to look in. When he pulled out of the hole his face was greenish beneath its tan and he swallowed convulsively.

"She—she had a full crew on board—" he reported.

Thereafter no one was in any hurry to join him at his vantage point.

"How many?" Hansu appeared below and started to climb.

Unwillingly Kosti peered into the wrecked crawler for the second time. His lips moved as he counted.

"—four—five—six. Six, sir."

Hansu called down over his shoulder, "Larsen, Bogate, Vedic, lend a hand. We want them out."

Reluctantly the men he had summoned scaled the mound of the tipped crawler as the Blademaster lowered himself into the machine. Even when they had the grisly job complete and the six bodies were laid out in the nearest shelter Hansu did not seem satisfied.

Five were Mechs and the Blademaster carefully studied their service armlets. But the sixth, though he wore the uniform of a veteran Mechmaster, was alien. And Hansu stood staring down at his crumpled form for a long minute after he arose from searching the torn and stained clothing.

"Vegan," he said so low that if Kana had not been at his elbow he would not have caught the word at all. "Vegan!"

And his bald astonishment at that identification would have been the reaction of any Terran. Of all the Galactic races the Vegans would be the least likely to associate with the mercenaries they held in the deepest contempt as barbarians. They were not openly rude about it as were the Arcturians or the Polarians, they merely ignored. Yet here was a Vegan, in a Mech uniform, perhaps in command of a Mech crawler—

"Sir—"

Hansu was shaken out of his trance by the urgent summons from Kosti now hanging half out of the plundered machine. "What—?"

"Cargo aboard her, sir. Looks like arms—"

The dead Vegan was left to himself as not only the

Blademaster but every man within hearing hurried back to the side of the wreck. Larsen appeared in the hatch, handing through a box which Kosti lowered to the pavement. They clustered in a circle while Hansu squatted down to break the sealing with his sword-knife.

Inside, rolled in oiled fabric, was a series of bundles. And the Blademaster lost no time in freeing the first of its wrappings. As the last strip of stuff dropped away he held, plain to their recognition, a flamer of Galactic design.

"How many more boxes inside?" he asked Kosti in a flat voice.

"Three, sir."

Hansu arose. There was a bleak look on his face. But a grim determination over-rode other emotion.

"Any way of telling where this thing was when the storm hit?" he asked Kosti. "Do these operate on route tapes the way a ship does?"

"I don't think so, sir. It has manual controls. But I can check—" He edged back into the crawler.

"Pretty far from Tharc, sir." Larsen broke the quiet. "And a scout wouldn't be hauling cargo—"

"Just so." But Hansu had already turned to the Ventur who witnessed the whole scene curiously from the doorway of the warehouse. "You're sure no spacer planeted near here?"

"None at the place we have used. Our mirrors of seeing would have told us—"

"And there is no other landing space within a day's travel? This crawler was carrying cargo. It would not have been carrying arms away from Tharc—not in the windy season. But it might have been trying to reach there from a ship which planeted elsewhere."

The Ventur's nod agreed to the logic in that. "This is a heavy and well-built machine. Those within it, if they did not know the full fury of our winds, might believe themselves safe in its belly. It is true that so they might try to travel to Tharc. But it is equally true that those in Tharc

—where the Llor know well the strength of the winds and would warn them—would not venture forth. Let me signal the Masters. It may well be that a ship has made a landing elsewhere."

He vanished into the building. And a few moments later Kosti brought discouraging news from the machine.

"They were on manuals when they smashed up, sir. No tapes. But I don't think she was scouting. The heavy guns were all still under wraps—two of them in storage cradles. She might just have come off a ship and they were driving her in."

"Why not land at Tharc?" Hansu mused. He brought his balled fist down on the edge of the broken caterpillar tread by his shoulder. "I want every bit of her cargo, everything on the bodies of her crew, anything which may give us a clue, brought over to headquarters. And I want it done now!"

14

THE HIDDEN SHIP

Though they found indications to prove that the crawler had been part of the cargo of a ship and recently landed to proceed under its own power—perhaps to Tharc—there was no clue as to where that ship had planeted. And in the end it was again the Venturi who were able to supply the missing piece of the puzzle.

The trader's communication expert threaded his way through the group of veterans to Hansu. He wasted no time in getting to the point of the news he had received from his superiors.

"There is an off-world ship grounded six gormels to the south—"

Kana was attempting to translate "gormels" into good Terran miles and making heavy weather of it, when the Ventur continued:

"It is set among the rocks on the coast so it is safe from the winds."

"How large a ship?" Hansu shot back.

The Ventur gave the odd movement of his upper pair of arms which was his species' equivalent of a shrug. "We are not trained in recognizing the capacity of your ships, Lord. And if it had not been that near there we have a small post

—" He hesitated before hurrying on, and Kana suspected that that post he mentioned was more a spy than a trader's station. "But this ship is smaller than that which used to planet near here, and it landed secretly during the first storm lull—"

"Fifty miles—" Hansu proved quicker at translation. "The ground between us?"

Again the Ventur shrugged. "Most is waste land. And there will be more heavy blows."

"But a small party could cross overland?" persisted the Blademaster. "Or would your people provide transportation by sea?"

The answer to the last question came first in a vigorous negative. Some trick of the currents offshore along that section of coast forbade landing except in the dead serenity of the calm season. As to crossing overland, the Ventur had no opinion, though he was courteous enough not to speak his truthful estimate of the state of mind of creatures attempting that feat now.

However he agreed to draw up a schedule of the storms and lulls which could be expected during the next three or four days. And Hansu had a second message relayed to the Masters at Po'ult.

The reply came that in the next lull the transports would put in, take on board the majority of the Horde, and leave a small party to make their way to the hidden space ship. It was a desperate plan, but not as desperate as the one they had faced earlier, the necessity for going to Tharc.

The Ventur liaison officer reported for a last check, comparing his set of maps with Hansu's rudely drawn sketch of the coastline and pointing out where the ship must now be.

"The Masters send their wishes for your success," he concluded. "Do you go tonight?"

"Not until the Horde has sailed," Hansu replied absently. His gaze roved over the men assembled in the room. Not all the Combatants could crowd in to hear this final decision—there were the sick and wounded. But who out of that company were going on the venture south? Kana knew that that was at the fore of every mind there.

He did his own secret choosing. Kosti, the small, lean man, had to go. Alone of the Horde he had knowledge of mechanics—had the know-how to take a ship—if they were lucky enough to steal it—into space. And Hansu—Kana was certain that the Blademaster intended being one of the party. But how many—and who?

In the end it depended upon a grisly expedient. The uniforms worn by the Mech who had manned the crawler were salvaged and cleaned and the fit of one of the tunics selected the man who would wear it. When one settled snugly across Kana's shoulders he knew he was in. And whether to be pleased or alarmed over that fact he had not yet quite decided before the Venturi vessels came in, to ride out a short storm and on the following day depart with the remainder of the Combatants, leaving Hansu and five men on the wharf. As the last conning tower vanished in the murk, the Blademaster reached for the reins of a waiting gu.

"We ought to make our first storm shelter before the next blow. Let's get going!"

The round dome at the improvised space field near the Landing came into view before the onset of the wind. But the protection offered by that one small building had none of the security they had known behind the massive walls of the warehouses. Together with their guen, the six Combatants crouched on the floor, deafened by the howl of the wind, wondering from one moment to the next whether that dome could continue to stand under the frightful pressure. The guen, flattening their bony carcasses as close to the earth as they could, kept up a monotonous whimpering cry which rasped the nerves of the Terrans.

After what must have been hours—but seemed to the dazed men days—later, they realized that the wind was dropping.

"Up with you!" Hansu was on his feet, applying his bat stick to the rump of his gu while the animal showed its fangs in a snarl of rage.

Within five minutes they were on the road, urging their mounts to that stiff-legged trot which left Terran bodies aching and bruised, but which did cover the ground at a good rate. They had been lucky—fabulously lucky so far. But when the dark clouds gathering suggested that they must take cover again there was no building to give them shelter.

Their only hope was a grove of trees, already showing splintered stumps where the wind had mangled them. Into this the Blademaster headed, producing the coils of tough cording which the Venturi had provided against just such an emergency. Each man lashed first his mount and then himself to the sturdiest trees. Since the wind blew straight from the west, they had a thin margin of safety against the eastern side of the trunks and there they dug into the mold, protecting their heads with their crossed arms, squeezing into the ground.

If their stay in the small dome had seemed an ordeal, this was indescribable. One fought to breathe, the battle lasting from one suck of air to the next. Kana lost all track of time, almost all knowledge of his own identity in that dazed, half-conscious struggle for air. Then hands pulled at him and he rolled limply over on his back. A palm smacked against his cheek, rocking his head on the ground.

"Come on—get up!" he was urged.

Stiffly he pulled his aching body into sitting position. Three men stood about him, and one of them held his bleeding head in his hands. Six Terrans had entered that grove and four rode out, leading an extra gu. Of the other two, they never saw one again, and the other they had had to leave as they found him, buried except for an outflung hand, under the tree he had chosen—the tree which had not survived *this* storm.

Would any of them last to the end of this journey, Kana speculated, as he clung to his mount by will power alone? Could they even keep on riding at the pace Hansu set?

But the rocky defiles of the coastline were cut by a river before the time to take shelter arrived once more. And in the cup of fertile land in the delta they chanced upon a Llor village. Trading on the custom of Fronn they knocked on the nearest door and asked for protection of the guesting room.

Within, stretched on thin pads, the Combatants dropped into a sodden slumber almost before they gulped down their rations. And when they roused the blow was over and the native household had come to life. Hansu returned from an interview with their Llor host and some of the shadow was gone from his eyes.

"That was the last of the big blows—anything after this won't be any harder to face than something we could weather on Terra. And we're heading right! There's been two crawlers through here—bound for Tharc."

"What"—Larsen was gingerly fitting his Mech helmet over his bandaged head—"do they think we're doing here?" He pointed to the inner section of the house. "Any questions, sir?"

"They believe that we're from the ship. I told them that we were caught in a storm and our crawler wrecked—that we're trying to get back. To them all Terrans look alike, so they've accepted that. We only have to worry when we meet Mechs—if we do."

They were across the farm land in an hour, making their way around and through the debris of the storms. Before them now lay a stretch of twisted rocks, scoured clean by the wind, over which they traveled guided only by the compass in Hansu's hand (which might not be accurate at all) and the map the Venturi had given them.

Gashed chasms which could not be descended led to detours and they camped that night in a crevice of bare rock
while the wind screamed in their ears, much as it had in
the badlands beyond the mountains. Only the threat of the
Cos was missing.

And twice during the gray day following they were
forced to take shelter to escape the buffeting of blasts
which could have swept them to destruction among the
towers of stone. A lengthy detour brought them on an ar-
duous climb down to the sea strand where they beat a path
through piles of slimy weeds thrust up in bales by the
waves.

Hansu was almost thrown from his seat as the gu he was
bestriding reared and screamed a shrill whistling defiance,
lashing out with its clawed front feet at a shape flounder-
ing sluggishly in the shallows. Jaws, seemingly large
enough to engulf both beast and rider, gaped. Kana, with
one instinctive movement, raised the rifle he carried across
his thighs and fired into that open gullet.

The creature's head snapped up and back as if it were
turning over in a somersault, as the water boiled about its
finned limbs. A horrible mixture of crocodile, snake, and
whale was all the recruit could think of as Hansu sent another shot into the writhing monster.

Its struggles took it away from the shore, deeper into
the sea, and the Terrans hurriedly backed up the slit of
beach, putting as much space between them as possible,
the nervous guen threatening to bolt at any moment.

It was Larsen who found the way through between two
giant rocks which brought them away from that cove and
out of sight of the struggling water dweller. Before them
now was a wide space of open sand, matted with torn
weed and other wreckage of the waves, including a battered metallic object which bore some resemblance to one
of the small Venturi craft. A draggle of carrion birds hung
about that and the Terrans did not halt to examine it.
They fitted their pace to their Commander's, heading due

south across the first good riding country they had found since the river delta.

The next gust of storm caught them in a narrow gorge. Sea water driven by the wind curled about the feet of the guen but Hansu kept doggedly to the trail and his persistence was rewarded with the discovery of a fragment of crushed stone marking the passing of a crawler. Heartened by this, he yielded and allowed them to hole up against the wind.

A steel gray sky had arched over them for most of the day and the coming of night only meant a general darkening of the gloom. But this time the dark served them better than light. It was almost as if the enemy had set a beacon to guide them. And that was no blue Llor flame which beckoned them, but the strong yellow of a Terran camp light.

Leaving the guen in Larsen's charge, Kosti, Kana and the Blademaster scouted ahead, dropping at intervals to crawl, alert for the slightest sign that those in the makeshift camp had posted sentries. At length the three lay on the rim of a small gorge staring at a splotch of light in which the tail fins of a small ship could be easily distinguished. No figures moved in the gleam and there was no sign of life there. It was Hansu who was ready with an order.

"Stay here!" Before they could object he had slithered away in the dark.

They shivered in the bite of the night wind, cringing from the salt-laden air. And below the sigh of that they could hear quite clearly the distant boom of surf. But nothing moved about the ship.

It seemed a very long time before Hansu rejoined them. And when he did it was only to order them back to where they had left Larsen and their mounts. There, as they huddled behind some rocks, he outlined his discoveries.

"—small ship—general outlines of a Patrol cruiser," he told them. "There're guards. Can't tell much more in the dark. We'll have to wait until daybreak and light before we make any plans."

Kana dozed off for broken snatches and he guessed that the others did too. Uncomfortable as they were, long service in the field had given them the power of taking sleep where and when they could find it. And dawn brought a lighter sky than they had seen since the beginning of the big blows.

The guen were secured by their head ropes in a side gully, though Hansu gave orders that they were not to be fastened tightly. And he did not need to advance his reasons. This was one venture from which the Terrans would not return. Either they would blast off in the ship—or they would no longer care about guen or anything else on Fronn.

They took the same way up the cliffs, working along the broken rim to look down on the hidden camp. In the light of day the beams of the lamp had paled and the ship was distinguishable from the black and white stone of the walls. It had been set down with the skill of an expert pilot in the center of a small, almost flat-floored canyon. And as Hansu said, it looked like a fast cruiser such as were built for the use of the Galactic Patrol.

In fact the Combatants were not greatly surprised when the daylight revealed Patrol insignia etched on its space-scoured side. Needle slim, it would accommodate a crew of not more than a dozen. And if it had brought in a cargo of crawlers, the living quarters must have been even more reduced.

"That's what we want, all right." Larsen breathed hardly above a whisper. "Only, how do we take her?"

Under a slight overhang of the canyon wall across from them was the plasta-cloth bubble of a temporary camp. And now a man crawled out of its door vent to stand stretching at his ease. His uniform was that of a Mech, and, as far as they could see, he was a fellow Terran. But a moment later he was joined by another, who, though he wore the blue-gray of a Legion man, was physically an alien. Those too long, too thin legs, the curiously limber arms, as if the limbs possessed an extra joint— To Kana's trained eyes they betrayed his non-Sol origin at once, although the recruit could not, without a closer examination, have said which star he did claim as his native sun.

The Mech made way respectfully for the newcomer, who tripped forward into the open and stood gazing down the narrow mouth of the canyon as if waiting for something important to appear there. And he was not to be disappointed for the shrill squeal of a gu carried clearly to the ears of both the men in the canyon and the hidden Swordsmen on the cliff.

A mounted party shuffled into view. The Llor sagged as they rode and their guen paced very slowly, their bony heads drooping to knee level with the lag of overriding. Yet Kana judged none of the Fronnian natives were soldiers—they had more the appearance of backlands guen hunters the Terrans had encountered after their forced march over the mountains. Their leader had a rifle slung over his shoulder—the rest were armed only with swords, lances, and the thick coils of rope about their middles which served frontier hunters for both a weapon and a snare.

The Llor chief swung off his mount and immediately dropped cross-legged to the ground, while the alien in the Mech uniform sat on a small stool hurriedly brought from the bubble tent by a second Mech and placed to front the native. As the rest of the Llor slipped out of their saddles, one or two to lie full length on the ground, three more Terrans appeared, grouping themselves some distance away. It was plain that a conference was about to begin.

It was a discussion which grew heated at times. Once the Llor leader went so far as to get to his feet and jerk at the reins of his gu so that that animal ambled unhappily into a position in which it could be mounted. Yet a quick gesture and word from the alien apparently soothed the native commander and he seated himself once more.

To be a spectator but not an auditor at that meeting was wearing on the Blademaster. He shifted his position among the concealing rocks as if his first choice of hiding places had inadvertently harbored a nest of Vol fire ants. But unless he could develop the art of complete invisibility, he was not going to be able to hear that group below.

At length the meeting came to an end. The Llor chieftain gave some order to the lounging members of his escort. Four of them got up, without any display of alacrity, and as they trudged across the space dividing them from the Mech contingent, their reluctance could be read in every line of their woolly bodies. While their leader and the alien stood apart waiting, they slouched to the vent door of the bubble tent. The Mechs went inside and returned in a moment or two with large narrow boxes, one carried by each pair of men.

Hansu had gone so far as to rise to his knees and Kana wondered if he dared give a warning tug to the Blademaster's coat. But those below seemed so intent upon what they were doing that there was little chance of their looking aloft at that moment.

Two boxes had been passed on to the Llor who received them in charge with signs of open distaste, but did carry them to the foot of the ramp leading to the hatch of the ship. A second pair of boxes were man-handled out of the bubble, also to be transported. Kana tried to imagine what lay within them. Weapons of some sort? But why put weapons into the ship? It would be far more logical if those boxes had been drawn from the cargo hold of the spacer.

When six boxes were grouped about the ramp the alien and two of the Mechs worked on the covering of one.

"That——!" Hansu's face was oddly pale beneath its dark

pigment. He was breathing in harsh, shallow gasps, as if he had been pounding up the slope. His eyes, glints of steel, deadly, measuring, were on the group. Alone of the Swordsmen he must have guessed at once the contents of those coffers.

Coffers—Kana's own skin crawled as he realized belatedly that the word was rightly "coffin." For the Mechs were taking out of the box what could only be the body of a dead man—a man who wore the white and black of the Patrol.

"But why—?" His muttered protest brought no answer except gasps from his two companions and an uninformative grunt from Hansu.

The boxes, now emptied, each of the same contents, were carried off by the Llor and piled against the wall of the canyon a good distance away from the ship. The alien was in command, directing the arrangement of the bodies in an uneven line.

Hansu hissed—there was no other way to name the sound he made with breath expelled between his teeth. To Kana the actions below did not make sense, but to the Blademaster the design must be growing clearer every moment.

Now the alien stood back, motioning the Mechs away, though the Llor still clustered about the ship as if examining the dead who had been so carefully placed there.

"He's making a record-pak!" The words came from Larsen and Kana saw that he was right. The alien, a sight scriber in his hands, was making a pictorial record of the scene—the ship—the tumbled bodies—the Llor moving among them. A record of what—to be shown to whom?

"A frame—a neat frame—" That was Hansu. "So that's their little game!"

The alien took several more shots and then nodded to the Llor chieftain who signaled his men. They scattered away from the ship with a speed which suggested that they were only too glad to be done with the odd duty their leader had demanded of them. And what followed was almost as mystifying to the spying Swordsmen.

Two of the Mechs struck the bubble tent, and the material, along with various bundles, was carried off. Shortly thereafter a crawler appeared from behind an outcrop but it did not approach the ship, only halted until the remaining Mechs and the alien hurried over and climbed through its hatch. Then it made off up the canyon eastward. The Llor waited as if to give the off-world men a good start and then mounted. But they did not follow the grinding passage of the crawler—instead they rode off down a side way.

The ship stood as they had left it, the bodies still lying at the ramp. And Hansu hardly waited until the last Llor was out of sight before he clambered down the side of the cliff, Kana and the others hurrying to follow him.

But the Blademaster easily outdistanced them and when they caught up he had already knelt to examine the nearest body. His face was bleak.

"This man has been shot," he said slowly, "with an Arch rifle."

15

IF BUT ONE OF US LIVE—

"But were they Patrolmen?" Larsen demanded.

It was hard to believe—in spite of the evidence and the identification taken from the bodies—that such a massacre had occurred. The prestige of the Patrol was too well established.

There was no possible doubt that the men had been shot, and that those shots had not come from the lighter air rifles of the Llor, the blasters of the Mechs or the flamers of the Galactic Agents, but from those specialized weapons carried, or supposedly carried, by the Swordsmen of Terra alone.

"If they weren't, they'll serve as well as the real thing in those pictures," Kosti returned bitterly. "If that Agent was taking shots of this it wasn't just for amusement. Can't you see the force of those pictures in certain quarters—scene of Patrolmen ambushed by rebel Archs—"

Larsen kicked at a stone. "I still don't get it," he admitted. "Why stage all this?"

"Alibi for going after us." Kana broke silence for the first time. "Isn't that it, sir? With a good story and those pictures the Agent could have us outlawed and we couldn't get a hearing anywhere—not even at Prime."

He wanted Hansu to protest that, to say that he was allowing an over-vivid imagination free rein. But instead the Blademaster nodded.

"That makes more sense than about fifty other explanations." The tall dark man got to his feet, his eyes fixed speculatively on the star ship. "Yes, they've set the stage here for something nasty. And it would probably have worked if we hadn't come in time——"

"So they're trying to put us on the spot." Kosti was inclined to be belligerent. "Well, what can we do?"

"Spoil their plan!" There was decision in the Blademaster's answer. "Kosti, get on board and see whether this cruiser can be lifted out of here——"

The Swordsman hurried up the ramp and Hansu turned to the other two.

"Burial party——" He indicated the bodies.

They performed that distasteful task as they had for their comrades so many times in the last hard weeks, knowing that when their fire cartridges had done their work there would be no identifiable traces left. They were engaged in sorting the personal possessions they had taken from the dead for purposes of future identification, when Kosti appeared in the hatch of the spacer over their heads.

"First luck we've had, sir. She's ready and willing to lift!"

Hansu only nodded. It was as if, having made up his mind to a certain course of action, he was now perfectly sure that fate would allow them to follow it to the proper end. Stowing away the Patrolmen's effects in a ration bag, he led the way up the ramp into the interior of the small ship.

The only star ships Kana had known before were the ferry transports of the Combat Command. And narrow and cramped as those had seemed, this cruiser was even smaller and more confined. The ladder stair, curling in a breakneck fashion from level to level, looked too narrow to give any climber safe footing. But they went up it——

beads on a string—with Kosti already disappearing through the first-level flooring and the Blademaster hard on his heels.

Smells assaulted their noses, oil, the taint of old air, or close living— They made their way up to the control cabin. Hansu pointed to the pilot's webbing before the controls.

"Can you take her up, Kosti?"

The Swordsman showed his teeth in a white grin. "It's a matter of have to, isn't it, sir?"

He buckled himself into position while Kana and Larsen explored the acceleration pads and Hansu moved toward the astrogator's position.

"Give you five minutes, ship time, to take a looksee around if you want, sir," Kosti suggested, perhaps because he himself desired a few moments' study of that puzzling board before he blasted them free of the doubtful safety of Fronn.

They made a quick inspection of the tiny personal quarters. The cubbys were in a state of wild disorder with clothing and supplies strewn about as if by looters. Kana picked up a tr-dee portrait someone had stepped upon. The oddly slanting eyes and triangular mouth of a Lydia I woman could still be seen.

"Nice artistic job." Hansu surveyed the litter with a professional eye. "Exhibit B or C—looting of quarters— done by the wicked Archs—"

"Do you suppose this was a real Patrol ship? That they actually killed Patrolmen so they could smear us with the job, sir?" Larsen demanded.

"Could be. Though it seems a mighty heavy argument to use against an outfit as small as Yorke's. We must be important—" Frowning, he turned back to the control cabin.

"Do you have a route tap for Terra in the file?" he asked of Kosti.

"Going to Prime, sir? I thought we were to make Secundus—" the new pilot protested.

"This may be a real Patrol cruiser. If they sacrificed that to get us I want to know why, and I want to start asking questions right at the top!"

"Real Patrol cruiser!" That sank in, and Kosti swung around to tap three keys in a case at his far left. There was an answering click and a small disc dropped into his cupped hand.

"Yes, sir, here're the co-ordinates for Terra."

He freed another disc from the apparatus before him and inserted the new one. "Strap down," he ordered.

Hansu stowed away in the second web while Kana and Larsen buckled down on the acceleration mats. A red light glowed on the board before Kosti as his fingers played over levers and keys.

"Let's hope we go up—and not off—" was his last observation as he pressed the crucial control.

A giant hand smashed down on Kana's chest, squeezing out air. Waves of red pain clotted into blackness. He had just time to know, before he lost consciousness, that they were lifting off-world—and not exploding.

Kosti was no experienced pilot and the thrust he had used to tear them loose from Fronn was greater than it need have been. Kana, coming back to life, found his face sticky with blood as he pulled groggily at his straps.

"The sleeper wakes!" Kosti looked back over his shoulder at the recruit. "Thought you had decided to make the trip in cold sleep, fella. Not necessary, we have plenty of room."

The ship was on Ro-pilot, to be guided through the warp by the tape Kosti had set in. They had nothing to do but eat and sleep, and live in the discomfort of return-to-Terra conditioning which would enable them to disembark on their own world without further adjustment.

"How long do we space?" Larsen had asked.

All three looked to Kosti for an answer but he only

shrugged. "I'd say maybe fourteen-fifteen days. These babies sure eat it up in warp. Patrol cruisers are built for speed."

Fifteen days. Kana, stretched in one of the inner cabin hammocks, had time to think without the pressure of immediate action or decision hanging over him. This mess was a nasty one—sinister. For some unknown reason that alien in a Mech uniform had set a scene, a scene which only their luck had spoiled. He was sure that the ship and its dead crew had been deliberately left to be discovered dramatically—for a purpose. Patrolmen shot with Arch rifles—on a planet where an Arch Horde was being hunted down. But why go to all this trouble? Why try to discredit as well as wipe out a Terran force, when the latter move was so easy and Combat might be led to dismiss it all as fortunes of war?

Such an elaborate frame meant that not only the renegade Mechs but the Agents wearing their uniforms had something to fear from Yorke's men. The story of the murder of Yorke and his officers? Hardly. They had no real proof of that—not even a witness's account which would be accepted at a formal hearing. Why—why—such a deliberate and elaborate plan to blacken them?

Could it be possible—his hand went half-consciously to the hilt of his sword-knife—could it be that the age-old stalemate between Terra and C.C. was to be broken at last? That C.C. was working feverishly to not only whittle down the Terran forces by attrition, but also to discredit them among the stars as renegades and murderers? Perhaps this would be their chance for an open fight—to stand against that condition C.C. had imposed—to prove that Terrans had as much right to the star lanes in freedom as any other race or species! It was a hope, only a thin one, but in that hour Kana sensed that it was there and he swore to himself that the next time he went into space it would not be wearing that green-gray coat which had been forced upon him.

The ship came out of warp, but they were still two days from Prime port by Kosti's admittedly ignorant calculations when it happened. A faint "beep" drew the attention of Kana and Larsen to the screen above the control panel. The Blademaster and Kosti were asleep and there was no one to explain the meaning of the pin point of light moving across the dark surface. Kana went to rouse Kosti.

"We might just have company—seeing as how we are out of warp." The pilot pro-tem rubbed sleep from his eyes. But one look at the screen brought him fully awake.

"Get Hansu—" he ordered tersely.

When Kana returned with the Blademaster the plaintive "beep" of the signal had strengthened into a steady drone.

"You can establish contact?" Hansu asked.

"If you want to. But that's no between-planets trader out there. We're on a cruiser course. Only another Patrol ship would be likely to cross us."

On a planet, armed, they would have known what to do when faced with a potential enemy. But in this space world, they might even now be needlessly alarmed over a routine happening.

"Shall I accept contact?" Kosti pressed.

The Blademaster ran his thumb along his lower lip, staring at the light on the screen as if he would have out of it "name, rank, and term of enlistment."

"Can that screen"—he jerked his thumb toward the vision plate—"be used for receiving only, or do we automatically broadcast when we switch on?"

"It can be one way. But that would make them suspicious."

"Let them think what they want. We need a little time and maybe some fast answers before they see our faces. Cut out the tele-cast before you make contact."

Kosti adjusted some knobs. A bright wash of color rippled across the screen and then they saw the narrow, high-cheek-boned face of a humanoid from Procyon. The skull-tight cap of a Patrol officer covered his hairless head and he wore the star-and-comet of an upper rank commander.

"What ship?" he demanded with the unconscious arrogance of a Central Control official. He could not see them, but he might almost have sensed he was addressing Terrans. Kana bristled, noting by the set of Hansu's jaw that he was not alone in that reaction.

"Give me the speaker." Hansu took the mike from Kosti.

"This is a Patrol cruiser, name and registry unknown." He spoke slowly, enunciating each word flatly in basic trade speech, trying to keep his native accent undistinguishable. "It was found by us deserted and we are returning it to the proper authorities."

The Patrol Commander did not give them the lie openly, but his disbelief was plain to read on his face.

"You are not heading for a Patrol base," he pointed out crisply. "What is your destination?"

"As if he didn't know—or suspect!" whispered Kosti.

"We are reporting to our superior officers," Hansu continued, "according to law—"

That narrow face appeared to lengthen in a sinister fashion. "Terrans!" His lips shaped the word as if it were an incredibly filthy oath. "You will prepare to receive a boarding party—" His face vanished from the screen.

"Well," Kosti observed bleakly, "that's that. If we try to get away they'll burn us down with their big stuff."

"Come on!" Hansu was halfway through the door. And, revived by his confidence, the rest trailed him. Out of the artificial gravity of the living quarter they pulled themselves into the midsection of the ship where the Blademaster unfastened a hatch. Beyond was an escape bay complete with two boats. But they were so small—Kana eyed them doubtfully, battling his dislike for being confined in a limited space.

Hansu paused half inside the nearest. "Kosti, you take the other. That will give us a double chance of getting our report through. If but one of us lives he has to reach

Prime! Failure to get through may—in a way—mean the end for Terra. This thing is bigger than all of us. Larsen, you team with Kosti. Set your tape for Terra—when you land make for Prime—if you have to beg, borrow, or steal transportation. Ask for Matthias—get to him if you have to kill to do it! Understand?"

Neither of the veterans displayed surprise at the drastic orders. Hansu lowered his body into the lifeboat and Kana climbed reluctantly after him. It required both of them to close the vent and seal it. Then Hansu flung himself into the cushioned hollow of the pilot's section and Kana took the other padded couch.

The Blademaster set a pointer on a small dial before him, checking it three times before he cut in the power which blasted them free from the cruiser. The force of that blast was almost as hard to take as the acceleration which had torn them out of Fronn's gravity. Kana's ribs, still sore from that ordeal, were squeezed enough to bring a choked cry out of him. When he was able to turn his head once more he saw that Hansu lay at ease, his cupped hands supporting his chin, his eyes fixed on the dial, though his thoughts might have been elsewhere.

"Are we free—? Did—did we get away, sir?" Kana asked dazedly.

"We're still alive, aren't we?" Hansu's ironical humor quirked set lips. "If they had sighted our getaway we'd be cinders by now. Let's hope that they will continue to concentrate on the cruiser for a few seconds more—"

"What made them so quick on the trigger, sir? The Patrol usually doesn't flare up that way—or do they? And that officer said 'Terrans' as if we were Lombros muck worms—"

"It shouldn't surprise you, Karr, to discover that some of the more 'superior' races who make up the C.C. Councils at the present moment are inclined to rate us at just about that level—in private, naturally. One doesn't boast of caste openly—that's too close to shape and race prejudice. But I've seen an Arcturian leave an eating booth before he had finished his meal because a Terran was seated as his neighbor. It's illegal, unethical, violates all those pretty slogans and refined sentiments drilled into them from the cradle or the egg—but it persists."

"But the Zacathans aren't like that—and Rey and Mic were friendly with that Lupan on Secundus—"

"Certainly. I can cite you a thousand different shapes and races who accept Terrans as equals as easily as we accept them in return. But note two things, Karr, and they are important. The systems where we are persona non grata are dominated by humanoid races and they are systems which have had space travel for a very long time, who have pioneered in the Galaxy. Embedded deep in them is an emotion they refuse to admit, even to themselves—fear.

"Back on Terra in the ancient days before the atomic wars we were divided into separate races, the difference in part depending on the color of skin, shape of features, and so forth. And in turn those races were subdivided into nations which arose to power, held in control large portions of the planet, sometimes for centuries. But as the years passed each in turn lost that power, the reins slipped from their hands. Why?

"Because the tough, sturdy fighters who had built those empires died, and their sons, or their sons' sons' sons were another breed. For a while, even after the fighting quality died out, an empire would still exist—as might a well-built piece of machinery set in motion. Then parts began to wear, or oiling was needed, and there was no one who remembered, or cared, or had the necessary will and strength to pull it together and make repairs. So another, younger and tougher nation took over—perhaps after a war. History progressed by a series of such empires—the old one yielding to the new.

"Now the races of the Galaxy with whom we have established the closest ties are, so far, not of our species. We like the Zacathans who are of reptile origin, we enjoy the Trystians, whose far-off ancestors were birds. The Yubana —they're evolved felines. And most of these are also new-comers on the Galactic scene. But—and this is important —they have different aims, backgrounds, desires, tastes. Why should a Zacathan fret over the passing of time, hurry to get something done the way we must do? His life span is close to a thousand years, he can afford to sit around and think things out. We feel that we can't. But we're not a threat to him or his way of life."

"But, sir, do you think we are to the others—the human-oids of Arcturus and Procyon? Their civilizations are old but basically they are similar to ours—"

"And are showing signs of decay. Yes, we're a threat to them because of our young pushing energy, our will to struggle, all the things they openly deplore in us. For, old as Terra seems to us, she is very young in the Galaxy. So they've met us with a devious design. It is their purpose to wall us off—not openly and so provide us with a legitimate grievance which we may take before the Grand Council —but legally and finally. They struggle to dissipate our strength in needless warfare which in no way threatens their control, sapping our manpower and so rendering helpless a race which might just challenge them in the fu-ture. And because we have fought and dreamed of the stars we have been forced to accept their condition—for a time."

"A time, sir?" burst out Kana passionately. "For three hundred years we've played their game—"

"What is three hundred years on the Galactic chess-board?" Hansu returned calmly. "Yes, for three hundred years we have taken their orders. Only now they must be beginning to realize that their plan is not working. I'm not sure that their motives have been plain even to them. They have played omnipotence so long that they have come to believe in their god-head—that they can make no wrong moves. For they have always operated against us under cover—until now.

"From the first we have had friends, and we are gaining more. And those worlds would ask questions if Terra were summarily condemned and restricted to its own system. Perhaps their own over-civilized minds shrink from such a practical solution, or have in the past. But where they could, they have cut us off. Terrans are not accepted in the Patrol—that is the service for 'superior' races. Traders do not allow us to join their companies. Even the war we play at is carefully denatured—though we still die— The most modern Mech equipment is years behind weapons the inhabitants of—say Rigel Six—already consider obsolete."

"But, sir, why this move with the cruiser?"

"Either some hot heads on the Council are going to push through ideas of their own, or they have begun to wake up to the fact that we Terrans are not exactly what we seem." Hansu turned his head and gave Kana a measuring glance which was sharp enough to reach into his mind.

"Why do you suppose that we have X-Tee training— that we make an AL man a necessary member of every Horde and Legion lifting off-world?"

"Why—you need liaison officers on other worlds, sir."

"That is the correct official explanation—and one which no Control Agent can successfully counter. But any Terran with the proper temperament for X-Tee is screened and classified from the moment of his first response to the tests. He is given, unobtrusively, all the instruction we can cram into him. He is urged to meet X-Tees on a friendly basis—under cover. And when he enlists he is given every opportunity by his commanding officers to widen his knowledge of other planets."

"So that was why you wanted me to contact Venturi, sir?"

"Yes. And that is why you went to Po'ult. We have long

known that we must have all the AL men we can get. And the wider their acquaintance with other life forms the better for us. If we must challenge C.C. in the open, we cannot stand alone. And the more races friendly to us, or at least with a favorable knowledge of us, the better. Incidentally we may be preparing ourselves for another form of service entirely. What if Terra in the future was to provide not fighting men but exploring teams?"

"Exploring teams?"

"Groups of trained explorers to pioneer on newly discovered planets, to prepare for colonization those worlds where there may be no intelligent native life. Groups, the members of which are selected for their individual talents, going not as Patrol nor traders, not as police or merchants, but only to discover what lies in orbit around the next sun. Groups including not only our own kind, but combining in a working unit half a dozen different species of X-Tees— telepaths, techneers, some not even vaguely humanoid."

"Do you think that can be done, sir?" demanded Kana, finding in the idea an answer to his own half-formed dream.

"Why not? And the time may not be too far off. Let us reach Matthias with our report on Fronn and he'll have a concrete argument to use in Combat circles against C.C. Suppose that all the Hordes and Legions now scattered up and down the Galaxy received orders to rebel. Such a situation would upset C.C. and bring an end to their carefully supervised peace. It would be cheaper to let us go our way than to tackle rebellions and uprisings on some hundreds of planets at once."

"I've heard a lot of rumors, sir, but nothing about revolt—"

"I should hope not!" countered the Blademaster. "Most of Combat are conservative. And we of Terra have lived a specialized life for generations. Combatants haven't much interest beyond the affairs of their own Horde or Legion. At Prime they try to locate the records of those with promise, to steer the men into enlistments where they can serve the cause best. But this mess on Fronn is going to bring the latent danger of our position home—to even the most hidebound of the Big Brass. Once they see that Terran can be turned against Terran with the approval of Central Control, that Mech can be used to hunt down Arch—they will listen to what we have to say." Hansu balled his fist and thumped it on the edge of his pad. "Time—just give us time enough! We must reach Matthias and he'll touch off the powder!"

16

ROAD TO PRIME

But for the two inside the escape craft time moved leadenly. They could only sleep, cramped in the single position allowed them, swallow ration tablets, and talk. And talk Hansu did, spinning in an endless stream tales of far-off worlds on some of which their kind dared not venture, save in the protection of pressure suits, of weird native rites, and savage battles against stacked odds.

Kana forced himself to concentrate on every word, as if he were required to pass an examination on these lectures, for by doing so, he could forget the present, sealed in a minute ship which might or might not make a safe landing on his home world. And he also knew that his companion was now sharing freely with him the lore he himself had spent years in gathering. He was being crammed by a master in X-Tee, a man who was explaining the central passion of his own existence.

"—so they had a sacrifice on the night of the double moon and we hid out in the hills to watch. It wasn't at all what we had been led to expect—"

A sharp "ping" interrupted Hansu as a tiny bulb glowed red among the controls. They had entered atmosphere!

Kana tried to relax. The worst nightmare of all, that

they would miss their home world and go traveling on forever into empty space, was behind them. There was still nothing to do—nothing they *could* do. Escape craft were entirely robot controlled—often those who rode in them were too injured or shocked to pilot any course. The tiny ships were designed to make the best landing possible for the passengers and they were to be trusted.

Where would they land? Kana stared blankly at the curve of metal roofing above him. A bad landing—say in the sea— But they did not have long to wait, that was a mercy.

"I hope we don't earth too far from Prime, sir." He forced himself to deliver that in as even a voice as possible.

"We'd better not!"

When they did come in Kana discovered himself hanging head down in the straps and, panicked by that, he fought his fastenings, unable to loosen the buckles. Then the Blademaster came to the recruit's rescue and got him on his feet. The rear of the narrow cabin was now the floor, and the roof hatch through which they had entered was a side door the Blademaster turned to open. They wedged into the small air lock, to be met by a blaze of fire and billows of stifling white smoke. Hansu slammed the outer door, his face grim.

"The breaking rockets—" he muttered. "They must have started a fire when we landed."

Fire—the ship must be surrounded by flames. But the memory of one of Hansu's exploring tales flashed into Kana's mind.

"Aren't pressure suits part of the regular survival equipment stored on board these things, sir?"

"That's it!" Hansu edged back into the cabin.

The walls were solid, a few experimental raps told them there were no concealed cupboards. There remained the padded couches. Kana pulled at the surface of one, and the spongy mat came off in a sheet. He had been right!

The base of each couch was a storage space and the suits were inside.

"They're going to be tight fits"—the Blademaster inspected the finds—"but we can stand them for at least an hour."

To climb into those bulky coverings in the limited space of the cabin demanded acrobatic agility from both of them. But they did it and the Blademaster set the temperature controls.

"Let us hope that the fire is merely local. When you leave—jump as far from the ship as you can."

Kana nodded as he screwed the bowl head covering into place.

Hansu went first, pausing only for an instant in the lock door and then vanishing. Kana followed as swiftly. He flashed through flames and smoke, and then he landed, went down on one knee, and regained his balance, to run clumsily straight ahead, away from the ship.

He blundered past trees whose crowns were masses of bursting flame, avoiding as best he could the pitfalls laid by roots and fallen logs. The smoke was a thick murk, concealing most of his surroundings. At first he had to nerve himself to stamp through fire, but as he remained unharmed, he grew more confident and did not try to avoid any blaze which crossed the path he had marked for himself.

Suddenly there were no more trees and he was out in the open on the edge of a cliff. Below a road cut through and in the center of that stood a strange unearthly figure he recognized with difficulty as the Blademaster.

Kana edged along the drop hunting a way down but the man below waved his plated arms to attract his attention and then brought the claw gloved hands of his suit to the thick belt which marked its middle. Kana understood and fumbled for the button on his own belt. Then he walked over the rock rim and allowed his body to float to the road, making a good solid landing not too far from Hansu.

Pity these things weren't equipped with rockets as well as antigravity, he thought regretfully. By the look of this stretch of wilderness about them, they were somewhere in the Wild Lands, and it would save a lot of time if they could just jet back to civilization.

Wisps of smoke still walled the road so they kept on the suits, not knowing when they might have to go through fire again. But the highway stayed in the cut where the bare soil and stone gave no foothold to the flames. Judging by the vegetation, they must be somewhere in the north-eastern section of the ancient North American continent—which at least had them sharing the same land mass with Prime. This country for almost a thousand years had been deserted after the atomic wars. There were tales of strange mutations which had developed here and even after the remnants of mankind came spreading back from the Pacific islands, Africa and portions of the southern continent, it still possessed wide uninhabited, almost unexplored areas.

Kana hoped that Hansu knew more of the country than he did and that they were not now just tramping farther into the wilderness. Maybe they should have stuck with the ship and waited for the firefighters who patrolled the wild areas.

It was proved that Hansu did know where he was going —or else had made a lucky guess as to direction. For the road sloped down to cross a wide river. And on the other side of the flood lay grain fields, yellow under the sun. The fugitives tramped over a bridge and then halted to pull off their suits with sighs of relief.

They drew deep breaths of rich Terran air with unspoken thanks. How rich it was Kana had never guessed until he had had to fill his lungs with the thin stuff of Fronn's atmosphere. Between the wine of the air and the warmth of the summer sun he was growing light-headed and light-hearted. He was home again, that was the most important thing right now.

"There ought to be a harvest station along somewhere soon now," Hansu said. "And we can find a tele-cast there. It'll call us a 'copter to reach Prime—"

"How far do you suppose we are from Prime, sir?"

"Not too far would be my guess. There's a wilderness section such as this just north of the center."

They marched along the road between yellow-brown fields which stretched endlessly over the horizon. A daring rabbit hopped beside them for a while, its nose twitching curiously. And above birds flew in formation.

"This was all thickly settled country once," Kana mused.

"The Old Ones were lavish with everything—life as well as death. They bred faster than they killed in their wars. Ha—there's a station!"

The building ahead was sheltered by trees and there was the glint of a small lake, an oasis of coolness in the midst of all the dusty hot yellow. Kana felt almost as if he were coming home, remembering his own summer terms of land labor. Perhaps they were already there—the harvesters. This wheat was fully ripe.

But there was no one in the building. Its rooms and halls echoed to their steps with that resonance peculiar to an empty space. Kana went to the food storage place while Hansu hunted the tele-cast. Beyond the back entrance was a strip of cool greenery spreading out toward the lake. Yellow and white lilies formed ranks along the stone set path which led down to the cupped coolness of the green waters and other flowers were banked in borders, the boldest of which had overtopped all boundaries to creep among the grass.

On impulse Kana went out. A breeze ruffled his ridge lock, thrusting fingers inside the collar of his tunic. Yet it was very quiet, quiet and peaceful.

Slowly he unfastened his tunic, shucking off the stale cloth with a feeling of relief. Then he groped inside his undershirt. He had come down to the water's edge by now. Long-legged insects skated jauntily across the quiet surface of the pond. Fish made swift, black, hardly seen shadows flitting in the depths. It was peace—it was home —it was quiet and forgetfulness. He poised his hand above it.

The Grace Knife, the sad dimness of its blade hidden by the sheath which had rubbed over his heart all those weeks, rested on his palm. His hand turned slowly. The knife slid, splashed into the dark murk, a swirl of disturbed mud marking its landing. But when Kana stared down he could see nothing of it. It must have buried itself, to be forever hidden from sight. As it should be!

He trailed his fingers in the water, and as his flesh tingled from the feel of the liquid, he knew a sense of relief —of peace. Maybe Hansu's dreams for their future would never know fruition—but he had made his own decision. If he went back to the stars he would not go as a Combatant—as a Swordsman of any class.

And being sure of that Kana rose briskly and strode back to the harvest house. When he opened the freezer and transferred food to the cooking unit he was whistling somewhat tunelessly, but with a very light heart. Luck was playing on their side, or at least had done so thus far. They had reached Terra, now they had only to contact Matthias at Prime. The rest of their mission might be very simple. He looked up smiling as the Blademaster came in. But Hansu met him with a frown.

"Could you get through, sir?" Kana poured stew out into soup plates.

"Yes. It was easy—too easy—"

"Too easy, sir?"

"Well, it was a little as if someone had been waiting for such a call. So we shan't wait for the 'copter—"

Kana put down the container of stew. "What—"

"What makes me think that? What made you suspect trouble just before that flood nearly trapped you in the Fronnian mountains? How did you guess the Ventur had a

hiding place in the roof of the warehouse? Sixth sense—
ESP warning? How do I know? But I know that it isn't
going to be too healthy for us to stay here."

Kana got up from the table with a sigh. "But, sir, they
can sight us easily in the open." He offered a last half-
hearted protest.

"There may be a jopper in the depot here. They usually
leave one or two at each station." Hansu tramped on into
the machine storage room.

Again he was right. Two of the round-nosed, tear-
drop-shaped surface cars stood there, covered with pre-
servative, but otherwise ready for use. It was the work of a
very few minutes to slough off that film with clearing
spray. And before Hansu got into the vehicle he caught up
a dull green coverall from a hook on the wall and threw it
at Kana, taking its counterpart for himself. Their Mech
battledress was well hidden by those and they could pass
for men from the general labor pools.

The jopper purred out to the road and began to eat
miles. From above, if any 'copter was on their tail, there
was nothing to distinguish their car from any other. And
many of the transportation men favored the ridge-lock
hairdress. The farm road soon brought them to a master
highway where they found company. Giants of the heavy
transport trucks winged them in. Hansu cut speed, content
to be lost in the procession which thickened as they drew
nearer to the port of Prime. Most of the trucks Kana
noted were carrying supplies—supplies to be sent off-
world to the Hordes, the Legions, out in the lanes of
space. For so long had Terra been geared to her task of
supplying mercenaries and their needs—what would happen if a sudden change came, if the Hordes and Legions
no longer had any reason for existence? How long would
it take to re-gear this world, to turn the brimming energy
of its inhabitants into other paths?

He found himself dozing now and again, and he was regretting that stew he had left untasted. Real Terra-style food—fresh—hot— No rations!

"What's the matter?"

Kana's head jerked and his eyes opened. But Hansu's shout had not been directed at him. The inquiry was addressed to the driver in the bubble control seat on the transport which had come to a stop beside them. They were locked in a line of stalled transports and passenger joppers.

The Blademaster got a garbled answer Kana could not hear. His face tensed.

"There's an inspection point ahead—not a regular one."

"Looking for us, d'you think, sir?"

"Might be. We'll hope that they're only after a hot runner."

A hot runner, one of the undercover dealers in illegal foods and drugs, was the type of criminal at which most Terran police drives were aimed. And if the Combat Police were in search of a runner, every jopper and transport in that line would be inspected, every man would have to produce identification. One glimpse of their armlets, of the uniforms they wore under the coveralls and they would be scooped up at once. Then too, they might be the objects of this general hunt.

"Can we get out, sir, turn off somewhere?"

The Blademaster shook his head. "If we tried that now, we'd give ourselves away at once. Wish I knew who was in command at this post. It might just make a difference—"

If Deputy-Commander Matthias was part of some mysterious organization fighting for Terran freedom, as Hansu had hinted, there must be others of a like mind scattered through the whole system of Combat. And so the Blademaster might claim the assistance of such a one—if he were on duty here. But the chance was extremely slim.

There were men walking along the edge of the highway,

moving up to see what was holding up the traffic. Hansu watched them and then stepped out of the jopper. When he joined the others he affected a heavy limp which quite cloaked the trained Swordsman's usual springy stride.

Kana ventured out into the neighboring field in an attempt to see what lay ahead. It was a temporary inspection post all right; the bright silver helmets of the police winked in the sun. But this was late afternoon. And with dark— If they did not have to pass that post until dusk— He turned to survey the fields, assessing the countryside for a promise of freedom.

Ahead they were setting up camp lights—stringing them along the road for about a quarter mile. But that illumination would not reach to where the jogger now stood. Then the steady beat of a machine brought his head around. So that was how they would keep the trapped in line until they had a chance to sort them out! A police coaster skimmed along the row of vehicles.

With eyes which had been trained from early childhood to evaluate such problems, Kana watched the three-man machine pass. He timed it with his watch. Yes, it looked as if they were on a regular beat. It was the most elaborate trap to catch a hot runner that he had ever seen. Which argued that either runner was in the super class—which Kana did not believe, for those captains of undercover industry did not travel, they hired others to take the risks— or the police were after other game. What other game? Them?

Some of the drivers who had gone forward were now returning, loud in their complaints. Apparently none of them had had any satisfaction from the police. Hansu was with them.

"There's a coaster on patrol along the road, sir," Kana reported.

"Yes." The Blademaster motioned for him to climb back into the jopper. "We'll have to do some thinking and fast."

"Are they really after a hot runner, sir?"

"I believe that they are after us."

Kana was suddenly cold. "But why, sir?" he protested. "Terra police wouldn't pick us up on C.C. orders—not without a secondary warrant from Combat—and it would take them more time to get that."

"Don't ask me why or how!" Hansu's irritation spilled over in that bark. "But we're going to be kept from meeting Matthias—that's my bet!"

"And whoever is able to do that," Kana said, "has influence enough to call out the police. It's only a matter of time before they pick us up, sir. Unless in the dark—"

"Yes, it *is* getting dark. That's one point in our favor. They're searching every person to the skin up there."

And they were wearing Mech uniforms they had no means of discarding or destroying now.

Hansu snapped open a small compartment and pulled out the district map which was part of every jopper's equipment. He traced road markings with a finger tip and then leaned his head on the back of the seat and closed his eyes, a deep frown line between his brows. The sun was almost gone, but still the line of vehicles before them had not moved. More and more of the drivers were gathering in the fields and words of argument carried through the air. Now and then one of them went back to his jopper or transport, probably to ring in to his employer on a speecher and report his non-progress.

"Can we make it, sir, even in the dark?" Kana asked at last.

"Get away from here—yes—I'm sure of that. But reaching Prime—that's another matter. If they are searching for us they must have Prime sealed as tight as a lifting spacer. Karr, what did they teach you in ancient history about the pre-Blow-Up cities?"

Though he couldn't see how ancient history was going to get them out of this, Kana obediently recited the few facts which had stuck in his mind for five years.

"The Old Ones built tower buildings—and they were open to the weather—no bubble domes. Wonder that the winds didn't wreck them—"

"What about underground?"

Underground? It was because the towers were unusual that he remembered them. During the atomic wars most of the survivors had lived underground. There was nothing ancient about that mode of life. There had been one lecture during his training, delivered on a hot afternoon when he had wanted to be elsewhere with a Zacathan he admired more than the droning Terran instructor. Under the ground—

"They traveled under the ground sometimes, didn't they, sir? Through tubes running under their cities."

Hansu gave a curt nod. "What are those drivers doing?"

Kana surveyed the scene in the field from his side vision plate. "Building a fire, sir. I think they're going to open their emergency rations."

The Blademaster tore the map loose from its holder. "We'll join them, Karr. Keep your mouth shut and your ears open. And watch that police coaster. We want to know when to expect its passing."

Though some of the drivers still grumbled, most of them now looked upon the halt as an unexpected gift of free time. Having reported in on the speechers they no longer felt any sense of responsibility. There was a general air of relaxation about the fire as they opened their rations.

"Yeah, I'm driving a time job," announced a tall, red-haired man, "but if the C.P. says stop, I stop. And the boss can just argue it out with them. He said I should try to make time on the road if we ever get away from here."

One of his companions in misfortune shook his head. "Don't try the river cut-off, it's not too good at night. Since this new section of highway was opened, they don't run a breakdown crew along there and there've been cave-ins."

Hansu insinuated himself into this group, assuming a protective covering of manner so that he might have spent most of his adult life pushing one of the transports. Another example of a good AL man at work, Kana decided. On Fronn the Blademaster had met Venturi and Llor as an equal, here he was adapting to another clan with strange tribal customs of its own.

"This river road"—he addressed the red-head—"is it a short cut to Prime?"

"Yeah." The driver gave him a measuring look. "You new on this haul, fella?"

"Just been assigned to Prime. I'm driving a jopper from the west, don't know this country—"

"Well, the river road's not so good if you don't know it. It's an old one—parts of it pre-Blow-Up—or so they say. Last summer there was a pack of fellas outta Prime digging around there, uncovered some old stuff, too. But it does save you twenty-thirty miles. Only it's posted as unsafe—"

"Unsafe!" echoed one of the others. "It's a trap, Lari. I don't care what the boss says, you'd better not run it in the dark. I've not forgotten that cave-in we saw. Big enough to pull a wheel out of the trans. That's what brought those digging fellas out—they had such a time filling it in they thought maybe there was a room or something underneath."

"Was there?" Hansu displayed just the proper amount of interest.

"Maybe. Fella from Prime thought it was part of a tunnel, but they couldn't clear it enough to be sure. But you'll be all right if you take it slow and beam your lights down. You have to turn off to the left about two miles from here—"

"Any more chance of a cave-in?"

"Could be. There's some ruins along it. I tell you, when we get past the barrier here, you cut your jopper in behind my trans and I'll guide you."

Hansu returned the proper thanks and in his own way faded into the general group where the talk now turned on the forest fire one driver had seen blazing that afternoon. A moment later the Blademaster's hand closed on Kana's arm.

17

PRISONERS

"The coaster?"

"Passes at irregular intervals now, sir," Kana reported gloomily. "We can't depend on it being elsewhere—"

"Tough. If you knew this country we could split up and try to run for it separately."

"Do *you* know the country, sir?"

"Enough to believe that I have found a way for us to get into Prime unseen. Once we are away from here—that is."

"What we need, sir, is a diversion—"

"Hmm." The Blademaster might or might not have caught that, for their conference was interrupted by a shout from the barrier and the drivers scattered to the parked vehicles. Some move was indicated.

Kana climbed back into the jopper, unable to see any way out of their present impasse. Though it was dusk, the fire in the field lighted this area and if they moved far forward they would come into the section flooded by the camp lights.

"Hey!"

Hansu leaned out in answer to that shout.

"You fellas with the joppers are to pull out to the right

—that's the new order. Wait 'til you get a space clear and then run out on the field."

Had the police narrowed their hunt to the point they knew their prey was in a jopper? Kana wished, not for the first time that long day, that he had one of the Mech blasters from the ship. Now he was without any weapons— even the Grace Knife.

But Hansu moved now. From within the breast of his coverall the Blademaster produced a three-inch tube of metal. Slowly he licked it all over with finicky care and then stuck it under the edge of the control panel. The transport just ahead of them pulled up several yards and Hansu nosed their jopper to the right, as he did so snapping an order to his companion:

"Pull up the rear seat pad and draw it over here!"

Kana obeyed as they bumped from the smooth surface of the road to the field. Other joppers were emerging from the packed traffic, before and after them.

"Ready!" Hansu set a dial on the controls and kicked open his own door. "Jump!"

Kana slammed back the door and flung himself out, hitting the ground with a bruising jar and rolling over, scraping skin raw in the process of his rough advance. Before he lost momentum he turned that roll into a forward crawl. And he was still making a worm's progress away from the road when the night split apart with a flash of fire and the sound of an explosion. The roar was succeeded by a confused shouting and the recruit cowered face down and motionless as the police coaster zoomed by on its way to the scene.

When that had gone he continued to crawl away from the light, making for a willow-lined watercourse he had noted earlier in the afternoon. And, though he expected any moment to be challenged, he made it safely, to tumble down the bank into a foot or so of cold water.

Reversing, he squirmed up once more so that his eyes were on a level with the road. Their jopper, ignited by the explosion Hansu had set, was burning briskly. The line of Transports was jammed tight again and a crowd milled about the circle of light and heat. It was a very superior and successful diversion indeed. Only—had Hansu escaped as easily as he had?

Kana crawled eastward along the stream. Prime lay in this direction and if he found the Blademaster again it would be along this route. He became aware of movement ahead—stealthy but assured. Hansu? Or some policeman who had suspected what had really happened?

The recruit unbuckled the belt of his coverall and prepared to use it as he had the rifle sling on Fronn. The rustling stopped. Then came the faintest of whispers.

"Karr?"

"Yes, sir!"

"This way—"

Kana broke into a jog trot to keep up with his commander. They passed far to one side of the point of the police barrier where the glare of the lamps eclipsed that of the burning jopper. And now they crept half in the water until the illumination was behind. Hansu kept to their creek road until a rise in the ground and a turn in the sweep of the highway put both barrier and road out of sight.

"Where are we heading, sir?" Kana asked at last as they sloshed soggily up the bank behind a screen of trees and brush.

"To that river road the driver mentioned." The Blademaster walked at a slower pace now, and he carried his right arm across his body, supporting it with his left hand.

"Are you hurt, sir?"

"Just scorched a little. Had to put that pad up on the seat before I jumped."

Now Kana understood. Dimly seen by those who dared not venture too close to the flaming jopper, that seat pad might be mistaken for two occupants trapped within.

"Can't I see to your burn, sir?" he persisted.

"Later—" Hansu appeared intent only in putting distance between them and the police.

And "later" was a long time away. The Blademaster's sense of direction and his study of the map brought them out on a narrower road which cut away from the main highway southeast. Since there seemed to be little or no travel along it, they dared to walk in the open, making better time where the footing was sure.

The moon was up when Hansu slowed to a stop. He turned as if on a pivot until he had made a half circle. And Kana, imitating him, saw what his officer had been searching for—trenches cut into the earth just off the road.

"Your flash—" Hansu bit off the two words as if to say that much had cost him real effort.

Kana unlooped his hand torch, set it on low, and pointed the ray into the nearest of those gashes. There was broken masonry at the bottom of the excavation. These must be the ruins the driver had mentioned. Hansu counted the trenches audibly.

"—four—five—six. That's the one—the sixth on the left—"

Kana's beam flicked to number six and, as it picked out the stones and ancient brickwork at the bottom, Hansu slid awkwardly down into it. The recruit jumped after the Blademaster, trying to keep his footing in the rubble of embedded blocks. Though he had no idea of what his companion was seeking, he knew better than to ask any questions just then.

This trench was longer than the others, running farther back from the road, but at last they came to a pile of loose dead brush and stones which marked the end of the excavation. Hansu pulled at the brush with his left and and Kana sprang forward to help. Under their tugging the stuff came away, to display a dark hole.

"What—?" Kana began.

"Underground ways—running into Prime—from the old days—" Hansu's answer was broken by curious pauses and Kana swept the torch beam across the Blademaster's face. Sweat trickled down through the grime and dust and under that Hansu wore the look of a man forcing himself to go on nerve alone.

But Kana sensed that this was no time to offer help. He allowed the light to travel on, back into the hole. And then he stepped into what was clearly a manmade tunnel. Under his boots were two strips of rust which must have once been metal rails.

These ancient ways were often almost death traps. As the Swordsmen advanced they passed side corridors choked with cave-ins and twice they had to dig through piles of gravel and earth. However, surprisingly, the further they went from the entrance, the better the condition. Kana could not believe that these hidden ways had been abandoned ever since the days of the atom wars. And his suspicion of that was confirmed as he caught sight—in a side tunnel—of some metal shoring, which reflected the beam of the torch, undimmed by the prevailing damp.

The main passage which they followed widened as more and more side corridors emptied into it. This must have once been a main entrance to Prime, or rather to the now almost forgotten seaport upon the ruins of which Prime had been erected.

"How much farther—?"

"Don't know." Hansu walked mechanically. "I've heard about this. We should be able to contact the Reachers— maybe one of their cars will find us—"

That did not make sense to Kana, but he did not challenge it. Who Hansu's "Reachers" might be he was beginning to guess—the mysterious underground within Combat of which Matthias was the probable head. But why the Blademaster expected to encounter them here was a puzzle beyond his solving.

They rounded a turn, a wide sweep which now embraced not one set of tracks but four, and came out into a space which echoed hollowly to the sound of their boots and in which the torch beam was swallowed in the dark. Kana switched on its full power and pointed the beam at the walls, sweeping it from one dark arch of entrance to the next. They were in a vast circle, the center of a web the strands of which led out to every point of the compass. And which of those archways should they enter? As far as he could see they were all exactly alike.

The unease Kana had always felt when confined in a small space began to operate now—although the area of the crossing tracks was large. But beyond the limit of his torch the dark had a thickness to it which was almost tangible, as if they were truly buried far below the surface of the earth with no hope of winning to the open air again. The dank smell he thought born of the damp and earth carried other faint taints—nose-tickling reminders of the far past. And now that they had paused he was sure he could hear not too far away the gurgle of running water.

"Which way now?" His basic dislike of the dark, of being closed in by tons of earth, brought that query from him in an impatient demand.

Hansu grunted but made no other answer as Kana continued to mark the edges of the circle with his moving torch beam.

Their problem was given a sudden and dramatic solution. From one of the archways, Kana could not be sure of just which, there came a humming sound, which began as a drone and grew to the proportion of a siren as it moved toward them. He grabbed at Hansu's arm, striving to draw the Blademaster with him in retreat into one of the other passages, wanting to take cover until they had a chance to investigate.

But it was already too late. They were caught—pinned in a wide beam of light which blistered their eyes as if it had been blaster fire. And from beyond the source of that luminescence a voice snapped an order they dared not disregard:

"Up with your hands—and stand where you are!"

With a sinking heart Kana obeyed. They were helpless, unarmed prisoners.

And that capture had only one logical conclusion—as he might have foreseen, Kana thought bitterly some time later. The wall facing the bunk shelf where he sat was an even, solid gray without a single seam or crack to distract his eyes or give a slight root for his imagination and so relieve the monotony of a time which was no longer divided into minutes, hours, days, or even weeks.

Even the indirect lighting of his cell waxed or waned at intervals which had no regularity so that he could not gauge the passing of time by that. When he was hungry he opened the door of a tiny chute beside the bunk and took out the capsules and plastic water bubble he found there. How they were placed there, he had no knowledge.

The continual silence was the worst. It was a thick deadening blanket which he fought until his nerves were tense, pacing the floor, exercising in a frantic endeavor to wear himself out physically so that he could sleep away a small portion of the endless hours. He was caught in a trap from which there was no escape. And the worst was that he knew the time would come when he could erect no more barriers against the silence, when the demon which was his own particular fear would close in to inhabit his mind.

The whole world had narrowed to this windowless, doorless cell somewhere deep in the foundations of Prime. The functions of the room were entirely automatic. Kana could be forgotten by his human captors, left here for countless years, and still he would continue to receive rations, the light would go on and off according to some weird pattern set up on a machine. But he himself would cease to live—

It was when his thoughts centered in that groove that Kana had to fight for control, make himself think of something else. If he only had a record-pak or writing materials— But for that matter, he might as well wish for freedom! He did not even know if he were already judged and condemned or was still awaiting trial.

Hansu had been wrong—so wrong—in believing that the underground ways of Prime were any secret to the Combat officials. There had been a C.C. Agent in the group to welcome them when they were herded from the rail truck at the brilliantly lighted station under the head-quarters building.

They had been taken without a struggle. What had happened since to Hansu, he wondered dully. His last glimpse of the Blademaster had come when they were separated at the interrogation room, just before he had been turned over to the questioners.

Those specialists at Interrogation were not crude in their methods. The use of torture to loosen tongues of stubborn captives had vanished long ago. Now after he had been given certain drugs there was nothing a man could conceal. Kana knew that he must have babbled every secret of his life to any ears caring to listen. When he recovered consciousness he had been here, stripped to the shorts of a prisoner, and here he had remained ever since.

Now he began his self-allotted task for the period after each meal, the attempted recall of all X-Tee lore he had managed to absorb. Sometimes he could really lose himself in that mental labor for as much as several minutes.

"Zacan"—he spoke the word slowly, trying to give it the proper hissing accent—"is a planet of Terra type. The continental land masses are mainly archipelagoes of islands. The largest of these is Zorodal. The citadel of Zorodal was first founded in the semi-mythical reign of the Five Kings, now a period almost legendary. Archaeological excavations have verified some of the legends and have proved that there are the remains of at least ten civilizations on the same site, sometimes with a lapse of a thousand years between the downfall of one and the rise of the next. The Zacathans are a reptilian race, allied to Terran lizard forms. Their life span is many times that of man. They are not aggressive, being contemplative with a well-developed interest in historical studies, producing many historians and philosophers of note—"

There was a click. A square space in the wall before him gaped like an opening mouth. Within rested a uniform case. For a moment Kana froze. Then his hands shot out and he snatched the case in desperate fear that it was there only to tantalize him and would disappear.

A uniform case, containing the complete new uniform of a Swordsman Third Class! His hands were still shaking as he began to dress. This must mean release, at least release from the cell. Was he on his way to trial—or to return to duty—or—? He was clumsy over buckles, awkward with the fastenings. But at last he was clothed. Only the sword was missing, the sheath at his new waist belt hung empty. And he had no Grace Knife.

He was latching the chin strap of his helmet when a second opening in the wall confronted him and he stepped through into a corridor. Base guards closed in, two before, two behind him. He wondered if he should be flattered by the size of that escort. But he fell into step with their pace, knowing it useless to ask any questions.

A lift took them up in a dizzy rise past level after level of headquarters' Administrative core. When they disembarked they were in a wide hallway on one of the staff floors. Murals of other world scenes where Hordes and Legions had made or unmade history alternated with windows which gave Kana his first sight of Terra since he had gone underground. It was mid-morning as far as he could judge, and below, the bay gave on the sea. Tradition said that the ancient ruins which were the base of Prime were merely the outer fringes of a once great city which had covered an island in that bay, a city which the sea had licked over during the atomic wars. 'Copters swung in heavy traffic between the buildings standing now along the shore. It was just the same sort of day on which he had first entered Prime to accept enlistment in Yorke's Horde—

But the guard allowed him no time to stare through windows or think philosophically of the past. He was speedily ushered into an audience chamber. There he found himself facing a Tribunal. High brass—just about the highest! Three of Combat's four Councilors sat there and the fourth and fifth members of the court were a C.C. Agent and an officer of the Galactic Patrol, a sub-sector commander by his badges. Kana stiffened. What right had those aliens to be his judges? He was sure that he could protest that, and be backed by the Combat Code. But, biding his time until he was more certain, he came to attention and made the formal announcement expected of him.

"Kana Karr, Swordsman Third Class, under enlistment in Yorke's Horde, place of service, Fronn."

Hansu—where was Hansu? Why were they to be tried separately? More than anything else at that moment Kana wished that he could have a moment's conversation with the Blademaster. For he had just made another and more upsetting discovery—one of the Combat officers facing him was Matthias—the same Matthias Hansu had been so sure would stand their protector, fight on their side if they could only reach him.

The faces of the Combat officers were impassive, but the C.C. Agent, an Arcturian—the brilliant scarlet and gold of his cloak somewhat garish against the green-gray of the Terrans—shifted impatiently in his chair as if he wished to speed up the proceedings and did not quite dare. While his alien companion, the Patrol officer, affected in contrast a vast boredom.

Then Kana saw what lay before the senior of the Combat officers—an Arch sword. That answered one of his questions. He had been brought here for sentencing. They had condemned him without allowing him a chance to speak in his own defense. But—how could they? The interrogators had had the exact truth out of him. These men must know of the massacre on Fronn, of that strange scene by the plundered Patrol ship, of everything else which had happened, know it as if they had witnessed the events in his place. How could they then——?

"For unauthorized dealings with an X-Tee race against all regulations," began the Combat senior, "for desertion of your comrades on another world, for the theft of a cruiser belonging to the Galactic Patrol, you, Kana Karr, Swordsman Third Class, Arch rating, are hereby declared unfit for off-world service. You shall be stripped of all Combat rating and privileges and sent to the labor gangs for the rest of your natural life."

Long discipline kept him at attention. Labor gangs for the rest of his life—the closest thing to slavery. But—a fierce, blinding anger uncoiled within him—he was going to answer those frozen-faced devils with a few home truths before they shipped him off. And he was not in the gangs —not yet!

When he spoke it was not to his superior officers but directly to the C.C. Agent.

"I've learned to know you for what you are—you and your kind," he said slowly between set teeth. The ancient blood lust which had once sent his Malay ancestors into battle swinging a bolo might have been thinned by interbreeding with other and more peaceful races but it was still there and rising in him now. "You may be able now to force Terrans to obey your will. But someday you'll pay in kind—"

The Arcturian's white face did not change expression, only now he sat very quiet, his long eyes narrowed into slits, a bird of prey preparing to swoop.

"How long"—Kana's attention was now on his fellow Terrans—"do you think you can cover up such messes? You know from my testimony—whether I gave it drugged or not—what they are doing to us out there. I"—he paused until he was sure his voice was once more under full control—"I gave Grace to Deke Mills after I heard his story. You know—all of you—what he had to tell. We are supposed to be fighting men—if only mercenaries selling our skill to others. Isn't it time we began to fight—against murderers!" He hurled that charge straight at the Arcturian, at the Patrol officer.

Kana was trying hard to pick and choose the proper words, to keep his red rage battened down. Then his mood changed. Why should he stand there mouthing statements which made no impression on their impassivity when he wanted to leap that table between them, to feel the Arcturian's flesh pulp beneath his fist? What was the use in talking—nothing he said—could say—would break through to them—would ruffle the composure of that traitor Matthias.

He brought his hand up in salute and wheeled to fall in with his waiting guard. Would they take him back to the underground cell? Or try to—for it would be a case of trying. He was determined to escape somehow, somewhere along the route.

Hansu— If they had given him life in the labor gangs, they must have executed the Blademaster! How wrong Hansu had been in his belief in Matthias and the new day about to dawn. With Matthias ready to betray them the rebels had never had a ghost of a chance.

They marched back to the lift and whisked down, not to the cells. Instead Kana was escorted to a small room just off the main corridor near some entrance to the building —he was sure of that as he watched the constant stream of Combatants passing in the hall. Except for a sentry left at the door he was alone—to wait— To wait? No, to act!

18

NO GUARD ON THE STARS!

Kana's mind raced as he assessed the situation. He was in full uniform, except that he lacked arms. If it weren't for the sentry he could simply walk out of this room, join the crowd in the hall, and leave the building, before the alarm was given. Once free in Prime he could find a way out of the city itself. There remained the problem of the sentry.

He watched the man narrowly. The fellow was in the act of suppressing a yawn as Kana first studied him. It was plain that he did not expect trouble from the prisoner. And this was no proper detention room, rather more like a waiting lounge for low-ranking visitors. The bench Kana had been ordered to occupy was cushioned and there was a visa-plate set in the wall to his left, out of sight range of the doorway. The guard's attention was often attracted by those passing without— Kana's eyes flickered to the visa-plate. Was there some way of using that? A little improvising— He waited until the guard's attention was fixed upon something in the corridor and then he jumped to his feet.

"Red alert!" he cried out as if startled.

The guard whirled, took one step in, glancing at the visa-plate.

"I don't see anything—" he began, and then shot a sour look at Kana as if angry at being tricked into speaking to the captive against express orders.

"It was red alert!" Kana insisted, pointing to the screen

The guard came all the way in, uneasily. If the visa-plate *had* flashed a red signal—then his duty was clear, he must call back at once for instructions. And he couldn't be sure that it had not.

"Keep me covered with your blaster," urged Kana. "I tell you it was a red alert!"

The guard drew his blaster, aiming it at the recruit's middle. And, with his back to the wall, his eyes on the prisoner, he made a crabwise march along toward the visa-plate.

"You sit down!" he snapped at Kana.

The recruit dropped down on the bench, but his body was tense, his muscles ready—

There would come a single second when the guard had to turn half away from him in order to push the question button below the plate. And if he could move then—

It came, the guard's head turned a fraction. Kana flung himself forward almost at floor level. His shoulders struck just behind the other's knees and there was a dull crack as the man's head struck against the screen, slammed into it by the force of Kana's attack. The recruit twisted on top, ready to carry on the flight. But the body beneath him was limp.

A little startled by such phenomenal luck—the fellow must have been knocked out when his head hit the screen —Kana got to his knees and hurriedly appropriated the guard's sword and blaster. But a moment later he reluctantly abandoned the gun. Only a base guardsman could go so armed and he would be picked up on the street if he were seen carrying that. He sheathed the sword—and hoped that luck would continue to ride with him.

The prostrate guard, bound with his own belts and gagged with a thick strip torn from his undershirt, was rolled back under the bench, well out of range of any casual glance from the door. Then Kana settled his clothing, donned the helmet he had lost during the brief struggle, and taking a deep breath, he stepped out into the corridor, closing the door of the waiting room behind him. He might have five minutes—perhaps more—before the hunt would be on. And now that he was again wearing a sword there was nothing to distinguish him from any other of the hundreds of Archs on the streets of Prime.

The streets of Prime—the sooner he got away from those same streets the better. This escape was all pure improvisation and it might work all the more effectively because of that, but he wanted to get away from Prime as quickly as he could. He covered the remainder of the corridor with the brisk strides of a man on an official errand and came out of the building on a 'copter landing some twenty floors above ground level. One of the dragon-fly machines had just deposited a veteran and was about to rise when Kana waved. The pilot waited for him impatiently.

"Where to?"

It was a pity he did not know more of the geography of the city. But he was sure that it would do little good to approach the space port or any of the transcontinent air ports—those were well guarded and the alarm would be flashed to them the moment his escape was detected. A little rattled by the pilot's demand he gave as his destination the only place in the city where he had been before.

"The Hiring Hall."

They arose and drifted west while Kana attempted to identify points below. Would escape by water be possible? There were only five surface roads out of Prime and each passed a patrolled barrier where vehicles were searched for smuggled goods.

"Here y'are."

The 'copter came to rest on a Hiring Hall staging. Kana gave curt thanks and took the lift down, heading not to the hall itself nor to any of the levels where the enlistment officers had their cubbys, but straight to the one place he thought would offer not only concealment for a space, but help in planning his next move.

The record room was as quiet as it had been the first time he had stepped within its sound-proof doors. One booth near the entrance displayed the light which signified occupancy, but the rest were dark. Kana punched for four paks in rapid succession, and with them repaired to the booth at the far end of the row. Feeding his paks into the machine he settled back in the reclining chair.

Three-quarters of an hour later the last pak had spun to its conclusion. So—now he possessed two possible answers to his dilemma. He removed the head piece but did not leave the seat. Well, at least he was given a choice. On impulse he went to the door of the booth to survey the room. The light on the other booth had gone out. But now there were three others in use. Was that suspicious? Did it show an unusual amount of study for one interval? Or was some big expedition being planned?

He could not see any way that they might have traced him here. The logical move for any escape would be to get out of Prime with the least possible delay. Certainly they would not expect to find him using record-paks in the Hiring Hall archives.

Two ways—his mind returned to the problem as he settled down again in the booth to stare unseeingly at the ceiling and try to plan. The sea way—he was able to swim though he had not had much practice lately. And the underground ways built by the Old Ones. Would the Combat police believe that having been captured down there he would be reluctant to try the maze of passages for a second time?

He was hungry. The carefully balanced prison diet had not been intended to build up any store of energy. And he didn't quite dare to enter the transient mess here, could not in fact without displaying the armlet which would betray him at once. First things first—let him get out of Prime and then he could worry about food. Out of Prime —the two choices were still before him.

And sitting here was not speeding him on his way. He had absorbed all the information the record-paks held. It was time to go. And in a snap second Kana made his decision.

The oldest building in modern Prime was the Histolaboratory Museum. Since history was not a subject popular with the general public on Terra, the building was never crowded. But, according to one of the paks Kana had just consulted, it had been erected on the foundations of a preatomic war structure. And so it might provide an entrance to the ancient underground ways said to feed all buildings of that era—a thousand-to-one chance. But he had been trained to consider such chances.

Kana gathered up the paks and left the booth. Three others were still occupied and he hurried past their doors. He returned the paks and went out, concentrating on presenting an unhurried, casual demeanor. Luckily the building he sought was not more than three blocks away and his uniform would render him anonymous on the streets.

As he went down the four wide steps to the pavement he was aware of a clatter behind him. Someone in a hurry. He quickened his pace and caught his thumb in his belt not too far from the hilt of his sword. If he were cornered now he would fight. Better be cooked at once in a blaster flame than live in a labor camp for life.

A hand clamped hard above his elbow, dragging his fingers away from his weapon before he could draw it. To the right and left grim-faced Archs had fallen into step with him.

"Keep marching—"

Kana did, mechanically, his eyes after one wild glance centered straight ahead. But they were not herding him toward headquarters. No 'copter settled down at their signal to collect guards and prisoners. They were still headed for the Museum.

Unable to guess what was going to happen now, Kana simply kept on between his silent companions. To anyone passing they might have been three friends on a sightseeing tour of Prime.

Just before they reached the entrance to the Museum the man who had kept that paralyzing grip on his arm spoke:

"In here—"

Completely bewildered, Kana turned in, the other two matching him step for step. They met no one in the wide hall lined with cases containing pre-atomic war relics unearthed in the vicinity. And no one appeared as they stepped on the down conveyor which lowered them to the depths under the street.

That sudden pick-up when he had believed himself safe had been a stunning blow, but now Kana was recovering, marshaling his energy to try another break at the first opportunity. But why had he been brought here? Could it be that they were under the impression that he was a member of some secret organization—the one Hansu had hinted about—and expected him to lead them to his comrades? Curiosity replaced surprise and he resigned himself to wait until they showed their hand one way or another.

More hallways and exhibit cases, gloomy rooms with displays or ranks of filing cabinets. Once or twice they sighted a man at work at desk or file, but none looked up or appeared aware of Kana and his escort—the three might have been invisible.

They marched on until they reached the end of that maze, a single large room crowded with machinery which probably was a heating or air-conditioning unit. Then the guard at his left took several paces ahead, threading through the machinery to an inconspicuous door which gave on a flight of stairs leading down into a dimly lit area where several small track-running trucks were pulled up at a platform.

There were men loading bulky packages on these, but they, too, gave the three no heed.

"In." A pointing finger emphasized the order and Kana climbed into an unloaded truck, hunkering down on a small seat. One of his companions took his place on an even smaller rest in front and the other crowded in beside him. The vehicle started away from the platform, gathering speed as it spun along the rails, and then whipped into the semi-darkness of a tunnel opening.

Were they on their way to Headquarters? But why travel underground when it would have been much easier to bundle him into a 'copter and make the short trip in the open? As the minutes of their swift journey began to pile up Kana guessed that now they were not only beyond Headquarters, but that they must be fast approaching the limits of Prime itself. He was completely confused over direction. They might have been out under the floor of the bay, or far inland, when the car came to a stop beside a second platform and his guards ordered him out of it.

This time they did not ascend but walked along a lighted side corridor into a place of regulated activity. Here, too, were series of file-filled rooms, and some laboratories with busy workers.

"In here—"

Again Kana obeyed that command, entered a room and —stopped short.

"Three hours, ten minutes." Hansu was consulting his watch. Now he turned to the man beside him, the man wearing a deputy-commander's uniform. "Pay me that half credit, Matt. I told you he could do it. Only a fraction slow —but entirely sure. I know my candidate!"

The other drew a coin from his belt pouch and solemnly passed it over. Kana shut his mouth. For the high brass

who had just dropped that metal token in the Blademaster's waiting palm had, not long before, sat granite-faced
to sentence him to a labor camp for life.

Now Hansu's attention came back to him and Kana
found himself measured with a critical stare.

"Rather lively for a dead man," was the Blademaster's
strange comment. "You"—he pointed an accusing finger
—"were blasted an hour ago when you tried to force your
way on board a transport to the Islands."

For the second time Kana opened his mouth and this
time he was able to get out words.

"Interesting—if true—sir—"

Hansu was grinning with an open light-heartedness
Kana had never seen him display before.

"Amusing dramatics." Still his explanation made little
sense. "Welcome to Prime—the real Prime. And meet its
governor—Commander Matthias."

"You pick up your cues well, son." The Commander
nodded at Kana approvingly. "Did that escape as smoothly
as if you had had a chance to rehearse it."

"I told you," Hansu broke in. "He's good enough to
make it worthwhile enlisting him."

Kana began to understand why he had been left in that
corridor waiting room at Headquarters, how he had been
able to trick the guard so easily.

"You set up that break for me," he said, half accus-
ingly. "Did you have me tailed?"

"No. Your escape had to look natural. We just supplied
the time, place, and opportunity—the raw materials as it
were. The rest was up to you," Hansu replied.

"Then how did your men find me?"

"Through those paks you dialed out of the archives.
That combination was a give-away—History of Prime,
Ancient Remains in Prime District, The Sea Coast, Map
of Prime—all asked for at the same time by one person.
So we just sent the boys along to pick you up."

Kana dropped down on a bench without having been invited to such relaxation. This was moving a little too fast for him. Easy——logical—— But everything Hansu said spoke of a city-wide net of surveillance, of a tight and well-functioning organization. What kind and for what purpose?

"And the labor camp?" He asked the first question of the many in his mind at that moment.

"Oh, there are labor camps right enough——supposedly established for criminals and malcontents of all kinds," the Commander returned cheerfully. "Only we differ somewhat from the C.C. Agents in our definition of both 'labor camp' and 'crime against the Galactic peace.' And those Agents would be quite surprised if they visited any camps except the two or three we maintain for official display purposes. Right now you're in what might be termed 'Camp Number One.' And we can introduce you to a lot of hardened offenders against the status quo if you wish. So you're going to serve the sentence which was imposed on you this morning——there's no getting around that. However, I don't believe that you will offer any objections to your fate. Hansu hasn't. Or do you harbor some deep, dark reservations, Trig?"

The Blademaster's grin grew even broader. "Not that you can see, Matt. I'll toil under your whips just as long as you'll persuade the powers that be to let me. I only wish that I had been let into the whole secret a lot earlier in life ——there're a lot of things I could have done——" He ended on a wistful note.

"What about Kosti and Larsen, sir? And the rest of the Horde on Fronn?"

"Kosti and Larsen earthed in the far south and have been picked up by our men——the C.C. Agents won't ever know about them. As for the Horde——well, that will take some arranging here and there. For the present they're safe with the Venturi——and I think we can make a deal with those traders. They're the sort we want to contact. We'll lift the Horde out of that pinch before those renegades and the C.C. get to them. On the other hand we can't slap Device down or spill all we have discovered about his backers. But the Venturi will be allowed in on part of the secret so that they will know you have not gone back on your word. Here in Prime Two we have a rather odd idea that promises should be kept—if it is humanly possible."

Kana felt as if he had been whirled through space without benefit of a ship. If someone would just explain everything from the beginning, carefully, and in words simple enough for his reeling mind to gather in, he would be happier.

"You'd like a few facts, wouldn't you?" Commander Matthias might have been reading his thoughts. "Well, this set-up isn't so simple that it can be explained in a couple of sentences. The whole project reaches back into our past—three hundreds years back. You know—if you asked an Arcturian or a Procyonian what he thought of a Terran, he'd paint you a mighty crude picture of a simple-minded barbarian. That has been our shield all along, and we have fostered the idea that we are rude savages of limited intelligence. It inflates the ego of the enemy and doesn't bother us at all.

"In reality Terra for at least two hundred and fifty years has been a double world—though that fact is known to a relatively small number of her inhabitants. One Terra and one Prime was fitted quickly and neatly into the pattern Central Control demanded and is a law-abiding member of their lesser confederacy, content with the role of third-class citizenship.

"But in the past hundred years one troop transport in every twenty which lifted from this planet was no troop transport at all, but a pioneer carrier. Men and women selected for certain qualities of mind and body—survivor types—went out in deep sleep to settle on planets our mercenaries had explored. On some of those worlds the native races had dwindled and retrogressed until civilization had faded almost to extinction, others were bare of intelligent life, or had dominant races, young, vigorous and humanoid with whom we could interbreed. There is even reason to believe that the latter may be descendents of the passengers of those legendary star ships which left this world during the atomic wars—though the people have long since forgotten their origin.

"So Terrans have been planted secretly on almost a thousand worlds now. On thirty our colonies could not take root, native diseases, adverse climatic changes, malignant life forms blotted them out. On six more they are still fighting a war for survival. On the rest they flourish and spread.

"Central Control has noted the decline in our planet birth rate, the fact that our race, which might have challenged the rule of the older groups, seems to be on the wane. They believe that this is due to their wise plans of the past, that as mercenaries we are bleeding our species out of existence. Only very recently have they had any hints as to what is really occurring. They may or may not have discovered that Terran Combatants, almost always hired to serve on backward, frontier planets, know of hidden colonies of their own kind—that our casuality lists often cover men who remain *on* the earth there and not *in* it when their Horde or Legion returns to base.

"We are leaving Terra for the stars just as we planned from our first Galactic flight. And now that Central Control suspects that, she is going to move against us. But she will discover that she is perhaps ten generations too late. One cannot move against colonies on almost a thousand different worlds, not and keep up the fiction of justice to all which must be maintained to preserve their carefully guarded balance of power."

"You are forgetting our allies," Hansu pointed out.

"The man in the field does right to correct the desk merchant at home," Matthias conceded. "Yes, several other young and vigorous races have fallen under the same ban against exploration and colonization which C.C. attempted to force upon us. And when these discriminated against X-Tees learned what we were doing—usually from our AL men sent to explain it in detail—they copied our methods all the way. There are about twenty of these worlds now following our pattern. This trouble on Fronn —the bald design of crediting a massacre of Patrolmen to an outlawed Horde, the betrayal of Yorke and his officers —is a blow back at us and may bring the whole scheme into the open. If so, we don't really care too much, we've been preparing lately for such an eventuality and we have our case far better organized for a general hearing than they suspect—too much of *their* planning won't bear the light of day. In the meantime—" He nodded to Hansu as if suggesting that it was now time for the Blademaster to take over.

"In the meantime operations shall continue as usual, both here and out in space. And as an AL man you're going to labor all right—just as you were sentenced to do."

Kana took it all in at last.

"I'll accept that sentence gladly, sir. When and where do I begin?"

Hansu crossed to the wall and pulled down the map hanging there—and the Galaxy was spread out for their viewing.

"They've tried to keep a guard on the stars and they have failed. No race or species has the power to do that, ever! You have a wide choice of operations, son. The whole of space is free!"